Belle Rouge
Book II

A Circle of
Secrets

by

Joyce Farmer Trammell

Vabella Publishing
P.O. Box 1052
Carrollton, Georgia 30112
www.vabella.com

Cover photo by Rachel Salmen.
Author's photo by Emily Maier, Emily Ray Photography.

Manufactured in the United States of America

13-digit ISBN 978-1-942766-11-7

Library of Congress Control Number 2016907879

10 9 8 7 6 5 4 3 2 1

DEDICATION

To Melba Harris for keeping me organized and dotting all the I's and crossing all the T's related to the business aspects of *Belle Rouge*. And to Judy Palsmeier and Alta Burnett for checking all I's and T's, etc. that I've written in the manuscript.

PROLOGUE

When we last heard from historical fiction writer Laurel Mackenzie, she had uncovered the secrets of Belle Rouge's first occupants, the Kilgores. However, there was one secret she had yet to learn. Her daughter Beth was carrying the child of Lucien Caulder, the man who believed he was the rightful heir to Belle Rouge.

It's now three years later and Laurel is about to meet more of her neighbors: Professor of Psychology Robert Ferguson, thoroughbred trainer Alex Jardine and former teacher Viola Flowers who is also known for being a psychic.

Laurel would tell us that she is at last truly happy because she's now married to the sheriff, John Miller. As she will soon learn, Miller has some secrets of his own.

The thing that holds steadfastly true is that, when one comes in contact with Belle Rouge, no one's secrets are safely kept.

CHAPTER ONE

LAUREL

It had been exactly three years since Laurel Mackenzie first turned into the drive leading to Belle Rouge. Even though the first year she spent in the house had been one of the most frightening of her life, she was grateful for all the wonderful things that had happened too. She had such amazing new friends in Eva and Jane. And then there was her beloved John Miller. Laurel assured herself she would have gone through most anything to have this man in her life.

As she drove past the maple trees, ablaze with their vivid red of autumn, she was reminded of some saying about walking through fire. Indeed, she felt as if she had been through fire, but it had only made her stronger.

Sometimes she wondered if there were a plan by some greater being that gave you little nudges, urging you to make a change. And if you followed them life would be better.

The nudge was almost frantic in nature when she realized she must leave North Carolina after her divorce, even if it meant she had to alienate her college-bound daughter.

The decision to move to Kentucky had come in a most unusual way. She had found a photo of her great-great grandparents standing in front of their store in Cedarville. That, she thought, was the clue as to where she should go, back to the very roots of her family. It was almost as if she was given the chance to start over.

Would she have made the choice to come to Kentucky if she had known ahead of time what would happen in that first year at Belle Rouge? All she had to do was think of John Miller and she knew her answer. Of course she would.

With the exception of Eva Farnsworth, Jane Miller and John Miller, no one knew the full story of what had taken place the first year at Belle Rouge. Things had happened so fast that Laurel sometimes felt the breath was being sucked out of her. It was as if she were careening down a waterfall, plunging into a whirlpool that spun her round and round. There were times she wondered if she would ever be able to come up for air.

Now those waters were calmer, moving in a gentler current. She and John Miller married shortly after she finished her novel. She felt safe with him in the house. He was a quiet man but, determined in his duties as sheriff. Personally, there was no show of affection from him in public, but he was passionate in his lovemaking. Whether in the early morning light or the darkening hours of twilight, if she reached for him he was always ready to take her in his arms.

During the daytime, if she saw him even at a distance, her body ached for him. She wondered if he felt the same. She knew in her heart he did.

John Miller had given her the feeling of safety she needed to be able to write the frightening account of what had happened to her at Belle Rouge. And now her book was about to become a movie.

Laurel doubted she would ever go see it. She never again wanted to feel those emotions, for there were times that year she thought she might be losing her mind. But Eve, Jane and John were there to guide her through the painful but rewarding experience.

However, she had never come to grips with who Barney, the handyman, and Nila, the professor from Savannah, were. There was no logical explanation for them to be alive in the present day. Eva suggested she look at them as guardian angels, there to help her with the revelations of what had actually happened in the generations past. That thought had partially put Laurel's mind at rest. But she couldn't help wondering if Barney and Nila might someday feel a need to return.

On this day instead of stopping at the house, Laurel drove on to the back field, the highest point on the farm. She had really never taken time to look at the property that adjoined Belle Rouge. But today as she stared across the field, she could see a two-storied farm house and a large barn in the distance. There was a smaller one-story cottage closer to her. Then a movement caught her eye. She saw a figure enter the woods that lay behind the cottage.

CHAPTER TWO

ROBERT 'SHINE' FERGUSON

Professor Robert Ferguson ran his fingers through the shock of gray hair that spilled over his forehead. It was his signature gesture, the one the students in his psychology class mimicked, especially when they became bored with his lectures. The professor didn't notice because he too was lulled into that place of oblivion with the monotonous drone of his own voice.

Over the years teaching had begun to feel like being on a treadmill—start at the beginning of the book in the Fall, get to the end by Spring then begin again the following Fall. He had repeated this pattern for over thirty years. Only when a new edition of the textbook came out and there was at least a little something new in it did he feel the jolt of adrenaline much like the caffeine in his morning coffee. But just as quickly as that rush faded, so did the newness of the textbook.

The idea of retiring came to him as little nudges in his thoughts. He always answered back by saying there was nothing else he could do with his time if he retired. He had never spent a year away from school since he was six years old. School was the thing that molded his life. He found comfort in the structure it provided. If that were to be taken away he would have no guidance nor purpose. He might just melt away like a puddle soaked into a dry and arid earth.

Truthfully, if he retired he was afraid he would only burrow farther down in his drab, dingy and cluttered apartment. If he died there who would even think to look for him? He had no siblings, no wife, no children and probably no one who'd even care if the body of the dull, old psychology professor who always ran his fingers through his hair had become one more thing to add to the clutter.

Maybe it was both the combination of the brilliant October sun and the extra-strong coffee he drank that morning that moved Robert Ferguson to climb into his dusty and cluttered ten-year-old Civic.

With no known destination in mind, he simply drove. Driving had become the only thing that relaxed him. His mind could go in neutral. He didn't have to think. It was almost as if he let the car go where it wanted.

"Good thing I never shared that with anyone else," he thought. "It really would be the campus talk if they thought the psychology professor were crazy."

About twenty minutes into the drive, he realized where his car was headed. It was going to the country and the farm where he was reared. He made no attempt to change the destination, though he didn't know why the car had chosen this particular place. But then again, the car always won out.

He still owned the farm and his long-time renters were prompt on mailing him the meager rent he charged them. He had never once raised the rent, and they had never asked him to fix anything about the house. He guessed they had taken care of any needed repairs. God knows he wouldn't have known how to fix anything. He couldn't even fix whatever this was that was ailing him now. What Robert Ferguson did know was that he was in a stagnant pond with no idea how to get out and onto solid ground.

The car bounced across the railroad tracks and his mind rattled back to someone he once knew there in Mountain View. Last time he'd heard about Alex she was still raising horses on the farm next to his home place.

"God," he heard himself say. "It seems like an eternity since we were in high school together. We really had fun in those days," he admitted.

He turned down the second road to his right, a narrow road that wound its way along the foot of the range of hills. He turned into the driveway of the old cottage. There was no activity around the place, so he continued on past the house to where the road ended behind the gray hull of the barn.

He got out of the car and headed toward the woods. The little boy, Bobby Ferguson, was headed back to the place where he found both solitude and pleasure as he was growing up. He stopped abruptly before he entered the stand of trees. He marveled at the vivid reds and yellows of the leaves. They were accented on the black trunks of the trees against a backdrop of a crystal blue sky.

Last evening's rain still lingered on the wildflowers along the path, sparkling when a ray of sun filtered through the canopy above, encouraging the droplets to fall like tears onto the mossy bed of green.

The broken twigs and the lifeless brown leaves that had already shed their brilliance crackled beneath his feet as he trudged along the old familiar path. It had been a long time since he'd been here among the trees. Just as he had aged, so had these old friends, but still he recognized them—the ones he'd climbed so he could perch high in the cradle of their branches and look down toward the valley that was his family's "kingdom." He chuckled to himself. "Like to see me do that now."

Today he was satisfied to lean against one sturdy trunk to see what remained of the farm. The old weather-beaten house was bent and broken from the years of occupation by generations of his family and now the renters. How he wished he could go back and once again see the smoke coming from its chimney, signaling that life was still inside.

The weakened structure would fall one day. The clapboard siding would decay and become a part of the earth, just as the physical bodies of his family had done. Their names were passing into oblivion—like the smoke that once came from the chimney. One day only the stone chimney would remain, marking the final resting place of the Ferguson family.

His eyes scanned for anything else that could give him a link to his childhood. He could barely make out where his mother's vegetable garden had been in the backyard, because it had been years since the rich soil had felt the prick of the hoe. Grass and weeds had long since covered the plot, but from this height he could see the outline. This relatively small piece of ground was what had sustained them with its bounty of food.

He could still see his mother in the kitchen, sweat pouring off her face in the heat of August, as she stood at the wood stove pouring that bounty into hot steaming jars. Then with a dish towel, she'd strain to screw the rings on tightly. He saw himself sitting on the kitchen floor, pretending to play with some toy, but he was really listening for the jar lids to pop as they cooled. Automatically he'd imitate the smile that crossed his mother's face. The success of her seeding, hoeing, nurturing, picking and preparing was judged by that final sound—the pop.

With pride, she'd let the jars sit on the table for several days where she and everyone else could see the fruits of her labor. But there was even more to the process. Storing those jars of tomatoes, corn, green beans and whatever else she had grown was what helped her satisfy a need to be prepared for the coming winter.

Now as he reflected on it, it wasn't just the preparing of food for winter that was important to her. His mother was always preparing for something. At her church she prepared herself for heaven. "In the Sweet Bye and Bye," she sang. "I'm Bound For the Promised Land," "Glory Land."

As he leaned against this tree trunk, he realized he was having a revelation. His mother was always preparing to go somewhere else, be somebody else. She was never satisfied with what was in the present moment. And there was always something that was coming, but whatever it was, it never seemed to arrive, at least not in her lifetime. His realization was—*his mother was a lonely and unfulfilled woman.*

However, the only certain thing, she always assured him, was Death. She was only fifty-seven when it suddenly and unexpectedly came to her. He found her on a weekend when he was visiting. He found her lying on the kitchen floor like a rag doll, he thought. "Did she go to Heaven?" he wondered. "She and the preacher always talked about it."

He never understood "Heaven," with its promised streets of gold and its white robes. What good was gold if you didn't need to buy anything? And white seemed terribly boring.

As for Bobby Ferguson, he simply wanted to go to Louisville when he grew up—and he did. He went to the university there and never strayed far, ending up teaching at the very place where he graduated.

"Bobby went far," he heard his friends and relatives say. But he knew he didn't. He just spent hundreds of hours sitting in a classroom either as a student or as a teacher. And he simply had pieces of paper that recognized those hours. He knew he really never "accomplished" anything, at least nothing that mattered. He always felt empty inside, like something was missing. "Was this what his mother had felt?"

After years of being away he was back in the country, wondering why he ever wanted to go to the "big city." He was wondering and wandering, picking his way through the woods, to the place where he first got his nick name, Shine.

He didn't really know if he remembered that day, or whether he'd heard the story so often that he just thought he remembered it. Now, here he was traveling backwards, going to the place where he felt he got his identify, deep into the woods, to the hidden place cut into the hill.

Not many people ever found the old path to Grandpa's moonshine still, but one day, probably when he was about five, Bobby ventured deeper into the woods than he had ever gone. All of sudden he realized he was on a different path. It was so hidden he never realized it was there. As he walked on, something inside him made him know he needed to be quiet. Then he heard them—low fluid voices, a stifled laugh and the steady running of what sounded like water falling into a pool.

As he crept closer, a twig snapped beneath his foot. The voices stopped. Through the leaves he could see his grandpa reach for his shotgun that was leaning against an old timber. He'd heard the men in his family talk about what happened in the old days when the "revenuers" spotted a whiskey still.

He knew he had to act fast. "Hi, Grandpa," he called in a voice he tried to keep from shaking. He dared not give much notice to the copper cauldron, but it was real hard not to notice the terrible smell of its contents. And it looked like the slop his dad fed the pigs. Right then and there he vowed that never a drop of liquor would ever pass his lips.

A joint sigh of relief came from Grandpa and the two men who were helping him. One was Uncle Jim whose ancestors had once been slaves to his family. He knew this because his Grandfather would often relate the family stories while they sat around the fireplace in the winter nights.

Once he'd asked his mother what a slave was, and she said it was someone who worked on a farm. He thought that was odd, since his Mom and Dad worked on the farm too. He wondered if they were slaves. Maybe Uncle Jim's skin color had something to do with the fact that he didn't own his own farm but worked for them instead.

There were a lot of things he didn't understand about life. The most puzzling was that everybody seemed to do the same things in this place. Everybody just worked, ate and slept and got dragged to church on Sunday.

But he did love the soft chocolate soil beneath his feet when it was newly plowed. He felt its warmth, he felt it was alive. The preacher had said that Hell was down below. Maybe that's why the earth was warm. He was glad there was a lot of ground between him and the fires of Hell.

He liked to lie between the hills of potatoes and watch the worms make tunnels through the loose soil. He reckoned they needed homes too. Once he'd heard his father say that, in the long ago, Indians lived in the caves that were in the hills in the woods.

He wondered why his people build their homes above the ground where the winds could topple them over. He'd seen it happen to a neighbor's house when a tornado came through. "Wouldn't it make more sense to live in a cave?" But then, women didn't like bugs and things that he knew made their homes in the caves in hills. At least his mother didn't like them, and he assumed all women were the same.

He also assumed that all females knew about Heaven and Hell, although his mother seemed to know more than most. She also seemed to know who was going to which place. All she had to do was walk down the street in town and she could tell which direction they were going, up or down. Once he asked her what caused people to go one place or the other. She said it was their deeds. Knowing that he wanted to avoid going there, he questioned her about the deeds that sent people to Hell.

"You'll find out about that when you're grown up," she replied without looking at him.

Bobby guessed he never grew up, because he still didn't understand why God would want to send someone to live in fire. He remembered the preacher quoting a Bible verse that said "God is love." It didn't make sense. Surely love wouldn't send somebody to a fiery place. The preacher also said we were made in God's image and that we should try to be like Him. But he had never seen God, so how could he be like Him.

He tried to make sense of it. Though, come to think of it, it did feel like his bottom was on fire when his parents had occasion to use the razor strap on it. He guessed that experience was the hate side. He never could figure out what was the love side. He'd never experienced that, he thought. The closest he could come to what must be the feeling was the times Grandpa smiled and patted him on the head.

If loving and hating was Heaven and Hell and human beings were supposed to be like Him, then he supposed all human relationships were also of the "love-hate" variety. Bobby would learn the term "love-hate" relationship when he got to college and studied psychology.

Thus came the second revelation he had on this day in the woods as he stood by the remains of Grandpa's still. *This "love-hate" definition of relationships had formed early in his life. He never wanted any part of those two extremes. It was probably why he had never formed any close relationships, especially with a woman.*

An unanswered question still puzzled him today. "Did my parents love me?" Neither of them ever told him so. He had nothing on which to gauge an answer. Only once had he ever seen his father touch his mother and that was on her shoulder. He was horrified. He had no idea what it meant. When they touched him it meant he was going to be punished. Did it mean the same thing with his parents? Did his dad hurt his mother too?

Bobby's body lurched forward as if some invisible weight had suddenly descended on him. A gut-wrenching moan escaped from somewhere deep inside him. Was he suppressing some memory? "Oh, God, surely not," he cried. "Surely, my father didn't cause my mother's death."

He had seen bruises on her arms, but she said she had fallen. Had he seen something else? For the life of him, he could not remember.

"That's enough! That's enough!" he cried.

At first there came the silence, a blessed respite from his thoughts. He felt his mind begin to travel back to a place of safety. Once again he was the little boy who had discovered the still. He heard his grandfather's voice as it anointed him with his new name, "Shine Bobby." The little boy had no idea that "shine" meant moonshine, but the name stuck. By the time he understood he'd been given the name because he had stumbled upon the still, he had already given the name a new meaning. *Shine* Bobby became his mantra. He was going to be a "special" person, a person who rose above everyone else. He was going to "shine."

Shine made his way back down the path. On this day he had come back to the woods as Robert Ferguson, Doctor of Psychology. Most everyone would say that indeed he had gone far. But why, he wondered, had he found it necessary to come back home and relive this part of his childhood.

He stopped dead in his tracks when another revelation came. Somewhere among those yellow leaves of October, among those tall black trunks he had climbed, was the little boy who had made the decision to "shine." Now as a sixty-five-year-old man, he realized something. *The light had gone out in Robert "Shine" Ferguson.*

Laurel hoisted herself onto the front fender of her Ranger. "I wonder if that man is the owner of the farm?" The house appeared to have no occupants; however, she had seen an older red car coming and going from the property, that is, until a few weeks ago. Now came the old Civic that had parked behind the barn.

She wondered if she should call John to see if he'd check on the man in the woods. "Hopefully, he isn't some trespasser." she said.

On second thought, she smiled, the Sheriff probably had better things to do than chase some harmless looking gray-haired man in the woods. Laurel glanced back at the man who by now had come out of the woods. He was entering the house.

Shine Bobby pried open the back door. The rush of stale air swept past him. He crept through the kitchen and living room and opened the front door. As he had done so many times in years past, he went out on the front porch, slumped down on the gray boards and rested his feet on the large stone that had always served as the step.

Robert Ferguson wished it was as simple to "air out" the human brain as it was the house. Instead his mind seemed to be holding on to old memories. But, he deduced, maybe he WAS airing out his brain. At least the remembrances were beginning to surface. Perhaps that was the beginning of the process of moving on.

He had assumed the tenants had planned on staying for the winter, but for whatever reason, they left, leaving only a scribbled note sent in the mail. They still owed him a month's rent, but Shine had no inclination to track them down for a mere $200.00.

Just then another movement in the distance caught Laurel's eye. Someone was going into the barn on the other property. "Guess he's the owner," she thought. "Then again, by the way the person's dressed, I'm not sure it's a man or a woman."

CHAPTER THREE

ALEXANDRA (ALEX) JARDINE

Alex Jardine shut the stall door and wearily made her way to the barn office. She plopped down into the tattered and torn leather chair. She was bone tired. Her knees and arms ached, but ten fifty pound bags of sweet feed were now neatly stored in the feed room.

Alex wondered just how much longer she could go on with this grueling work she had readily taken upon herself. She had what she had wanted ever since she was a child—a stable filled with thoroughbred broodmares and their babies.

"Why had she chosen to do this alone?" It had never entered her mind until now. Here she was near the age when everyone else was retiring and she was still trying to do what she had done since she was in her twenties.

Not only was raising horses back-breaking physically, but mentally it had taken its toll. She let herself get too close to her horses. She had sold some yearlings, watched them go to the track, watched them go to the winner's circle and watched them break down.

These were her children and she couldn't always protect them. But a horse safe in a pasture was not one who could put money in her checking account. She had to sell them to make ends meet, and sometimes they sacrificed their lives in order for her to do this.

"Hell, they weren't always safe here on the farm," she remembered. There were freak accidents here—a leg trapped under a stall door, a neck broken when a halter got caught on a fence post. Because of her mistakes, leaving a halter on in the field, a door too high off the ground, these horses had died. It was a hell of a business.

Alex wondered what her mother would say if she could hear the words she had added to her vocabulary, words she had learned while working at the race track. To make ends meet she'd taken a job as an outrider at the training track. It was an exciting job to be able to catch runaways or take a fractious two-year-old to the gate. Sometimes she even got a tip when one of those horses won. But not many trainers could tip. They needed all their money just to make ends meet.

HE flashed into her mind. She'd tried hard to keep him out of her thoughts, but in the quiet times she realized he was still there, the only man she felt she ever loved. She knew it from the first time she saw him.

He was a new trainer stabled at a barn next to the gate leading to the track. She was on a break one day when she ambled over to the barn to talk to a friend who was stabled in the same barn. Alex was looking down the shed row when he came around the corner on a big chestnut mare who was full of fire. Their eyes met when he was just a few feet away. It was his smile that captivated her, and that kind of a smile was rare in this business.

She began taking his horses to the track, helping him with his billing, going to his apartment at night, always secretly. He told her the track was a place filled with gossip and she knew it, but that wasn't the main reason he demanded they keep their relationship a secret. Some months after the affair began she found out he had a wife in Florida where he stabled in the winter.

She denied herself the feeling of heartbreak. What was the use? These relationships were common at the track. Alex just never thought she'd be caught up in one.

But then nothing seemed to last very long at the track. People were here today, gone tomorrow to some other race meet.

It also seemed to be the motto of racing in general. One day you have an excellent racing prospect; the next day the animal injures itself in some stupid way. It's just the nature of the business. It's a roller coaster ride. Why shouldn't relationships in this atmosphere be the same way?

Alex Jardine simply made sure she didn't repeat this mistake. She had vowed to hold all men at arm's length. However, there was some satisfaction in the fact that she had the reputation of being unattainable. There was nothing that stimulated the men in her world of racing more than the fact that they loved a challenge, whether it be from trying to get a horse to the winner's circle or get a woman into their bed.

"That's enough of that, old girl," she said as she twisted her body trying to alleviate some of the pain that was racking it. However, there was one great success story in her career.

She smiled as she remembered the little chestnut filly. She was well put together, seemingly preferring to be a pet rather than being a race horse. But one day Alex was sitting in front of the barn, taking a breather from mucking out the stalls. The little chestnut had been in a paddock with another yearling, and Alex had just put her back into the large pasture with several other yearlings and mares.

Alex was once again about to make an error in her judgment. She assumed the filly was running away from the other horses because she was afraid of them. She changed her mind a short time later when she put the filly and her paddock mate into their stalls so the vet could give them their shots.

"Which one do we let out first?" the vet asked.

"Take the bay," she replied.

By the time Alex got to the chestnut filly, she could easily see the filly was upset. "Nothing new," she thought. "She's always going to need her buddy. She'll be no good at the track."

When Alex opened the stall door she saw a horse she didn't recognize. The filly was standing on her hind legs. But it was the fire in the horse's eyes that told the story.

The vet was quickly at her side, grinning. "I don't believe there's any more doubt about her having the desire to win."

But Alex knew she'd have to sell her to make ends meet. The filly was small and from the first crop of a stakes-placed stallion. She sold her for ten thousand at the Fall sale. The money paid a few of her bills, but the filly went on to win over a million dollars with her new owner.

On the racing form Alex's name did appear as breeder of the filly, and she was proud. She wanted to put a big sign on the farm fence next to the road so everyone could see. "JARDINE FARM - HOME OF THE WORLD CHAMPION SPRINTING FILLY OF 1999." But she didn't. Her judgment came from her mother. "If you brag about your accomplishments, you'll have to suffer the consequences."

Alex didn't choose to suffer any more. Her body was suffering enough.

CHAPTER FOUR

ALEX AND BOBBY

There were several revelations Shine Bobby had that day in the woods, but he still had so many questions that remained unanswered. Was it really Shine Bobby who wanted to go to college, or was that his father's dream? He'd heard the bitterness in his father's voice as he talked about having to quit school in the eighth grade to help support the family. He was hell-bent that his son would go to college.

Shine wondered why he hadn't gone farther away to school? A snippet of a conversation between his parents slipped into his conscious mind. His mother was saying, "We can't afford to send him away to school."

"Alright," his father retaliated, "we'll send him to the university in Louisville."

So the compromise was reached. Shine could go to college only if he stayed close to home. This concession his father made to his mother settled his destiny. But at the time he didn't care where he went, just so he didn't have to stay on the farm.

Shine wondered why he always accepted his parents' decisions. Robert Ferguson, professor of psychology, knew the answer. He was a "pleaser." He did have that one talent, he admitted. He could see what other people wanted of him. Therefore, he was totally unaware of what he wanted.

Was that why he was back here in Shine Bobby's world? Was he here to find out what he had really wanted in life? Of course he was. The real question was: Is it too late?

Alex stretched her legs and let out a soft moan as she tried to find a more comfortable position in the old chair. How much longer could she go on with this demanding work that was now piling up on her? There were fences to mend, stalls to mend, a house to mend and horses to mend. But what about Alex? When was it going to be time for her to mend? Her body was telling her it should be soon.

Slowly she ambled toward the house and climbed the steps, trying to ignore the sharp pain in her left knee. She pulled on the screen door and it flew back against the wall, the worn-out spring refusing to bring it back.

"Just one more thing that needs to be fixed," she muttered, leaving it flapping against the wall. She knew she'd have to close it later, especially if the wind picked up, but right now she simply didn't have the energy.

Alex was hungry. The refrigerator harbored her staples. Milk, juice, diet cola, lunch meat and bread. She never sat down for a meal, unless there was the rare occasion when she let herself go the track kitchen before she came home. Even there she never tarried long. She wolfed down the food and popped an antacid in her mouth with the final gulp of water, surmising that she could make a fortune if she had an antacid stand at the track. Better yet, she could supply the generic form. No one at the track had enough money to buy a name brand.

Her routine seldom varied. The sandwich devoured and diet cola in hand, she'd plop down in front of the television. Her only luxury was dish TV. It had the racing channels.

Alex, remote in hand, flipped back and forth between the channels, unable to concentrate. She leaned her head against the recliner. It wouldn't be long before she'd be asleep. "My God, she muttered. "What have I become?"

"But this is what I asked for," she reminded herself again. "A place of my own where I could raise horses. I got exactly what I asked for. But I didn't want to kill myself doing it. Besides, what do I have to show for it? I've spent every bit of the money I've made just to keep my head above water."

Alex felt a tear trickle down her cheek. "I love my horses, but I have absolutely nothing to show for my life's work. No man who loves me, no children to take care of me and no really good horses racing in my name."

She heard the screen door bang against the house. "Damnit," she exclaimed as she made her way across the room. When she reached out to pull it to, she saw the figure of a man sitting on the front porch of the Ferguson house. "I wonder what Shine Bobby's doing here?"

CHAPTER FIVE

NEW FRIENDS

When Laurel got back to the house, Eva and Jane were waiting for her. "Who owns the two farms just east of Belle Rouge?" she asked.

"The one that adjoins this farm is the Ferguson place," Jane offered. "There have been renters in if for a few years, but I hear they've moved out. Why do you ask?"

"I saw a gray haired man walk into the woods behind the house."

Eva laughed. "That had to be Professor Robert Ferguson. He hasn't been here for years. Guess he's too busy at the university."

"We used to call him Shine Bobby," Jane snickered. "The story goes that his grandfather named him that after he came upon him making moonshine in the woods."

"And who owns the farm just beyond the Ferguson place?"

"That would be Alex Jardine," Eva shook her head. "Rather sad story. Her parents died when Alex was in her early twenties. She's been taking care of the place by herself ever since."

"She works at the training track in Louisville, and she trains a few horses now and then," Jane added.

Laurel went to the fridge and took out a pitcher of iced tea, poured three glasses and sat down at the kitchen table.

Eva and Jane took their seats and waited for Laurel to speak again. They knew something was brewing in her head.

Finally, Laurel said, "You know, after Karen and Allen moved I had no one to train my horse. Now he's just doing nothing here on this farm. Crimson Flame never got a chance to race after his injury. He looks so forlorn, so alone in the pasture.

I think I might speak with Alex Jardine. Have you made out the invitations for the book signing yet?"

"No, that's what we're here for," Jane answered. "Would you care to invite Alex to the book signing, though I doubt she'd attend."

"Do you think she's a friend of Robert Ferguson?"

"We all went to high school together. They may have kept in touch."

"Good," said Laurel. "Send an invitation to both, and tell them the other is invited. Now, she changed the subject. "Have you both thought about my offer of turning Belle Rouge, at least part of the year, into a Bed and Breakfast?"

"We have," both Eva and Jane again answered in unison.

"Jane and I think we could do a booming business with your book and the movie coming out. I bet we'd even attract some ghost hunters."

"And," Jane hesitated for a moment. "Do you think we could ask a friend of ours to help us?"

"Hire whomever you want," Laurel answered.

"Well," now it was Eva who hesitated. "She's a bit eccentric and …"

"Come on," Laurel grinned. "Spit it out."

"Viola reads cards like I do."

"Oh, good. Now we have a coven of witches along with the ghosts at Belle Rouge. That ought to pack the house with guests," Laurel quipped. "What's Viola's last name? I haven't heard either of you speak of her before."

"It's Viola Flowers," Jane answered. "She and I taught together at the high school. She was the music teacher. I ran into her at the grocery the other day, and I get the feeling she's like us—a bit bored with retirement."

"Wait," Laurel cried, "I have an even better idea. Let's have a dinner party after the book signing, and we can all get to know one another. Invite all three—Alex Jardine, Robert Ferguson and Viola Flowers. Maybe we could even read cards, play the Ouija board, have a séance," Laurel laughed.

Shine Bobby glanced back toward the woods. Soon only a few leaves would remain on the trees. Even when they were bare they continued to hide his grandfather's still. "He was a clever man," Shine deduced. How he wished he were clever too.

He, Dr. Robert Ferguson, wasn't. He only had book knowledge, but his grandfather had some sort of connection to nature, to life. He seemed to understand how it worked. Dr. Robert Ferguson didn't.

Shine Bobby had chosen his field in academia, but he couldn't pinpoint when he had chosen it. He just seemed to fall into it. Life at the university simply was comfortable for him. It was easy for the student to pass into the role of professor.

As Alex watched she saw Shine Bobby get in his old Civic and head down the road toward her house. When he pulled into her driveway she went out to meet him. "What brings you back to your farm, Bobby?" she asked.

"My renters have moved," he replied. "I thought I'd better come by and see the condition of the house."

"Did they do any damage?" she asked.

"Actually they left it in good shape."

Alex felt that was only part of the story. "How about a cup of coffee?

"Yes, I'd like that," he smiled, realizing that it had been quite some time since he had even felt like smiling.

He had followed Alex's career with the horses. She had been quite successful, in his opinion. He wondered how it felt to be so passionate about one's career.

He followed her into the house, carefully pulling the screen door shut behind him.

"Sorry the place is such a mess," she was saying. "I never was much about the domestic stuff."

"You should see my apartment," he responded. "I don't even remember when I last straightened things. I've got stacks of books everywhere."

"I could see you doing that," she laughed. "I'm really glad you stopped, Shine. I can't remember the last time we saw each other."

"You still remember my nickname."

"Of course I do. That's who you were - Shine Bobby," she said, reaching into the cabinet for two mugs. "I'm afraid this coffee's pretty strong. It's been sitting here for a while. I've got this bad habit of drinking it all day long. It's sort of a racetrack thing. The coffee's always on."

She offered him the recliner, but he chose the couch, realizing it was evident that the chair was Alex's domain. "So, how's racing going?" he asked.

Alex sighed. "Not too well right now. I'm taking a break, just trying to get a couple of babies weaned."

"Do you have any good ones?" he asked.

"One of them really looks grand. I'm hoping he'll bring a good price at next year's yearling sale. He has good breeding."

"What is the breeding?"

Alex laughed. "Would you even know if I told you?"

"Try me. I might know more than you think."

Alex Jardine was in her element when it came to the breeding of the thoroughbred. The colt was a grandson of one of the best sires and out of one of Alex's mares who had been an allowance winner at Churchill Downs. The second dam had produced two stakes-placed winners. The third dam was a multiple stakes winner.

The colt was well balanced and she really liked the way he moved. In fact, his breeding contained the names of two Kentucky Derby winners.

When Alex paused for a breath she saw that Shine Bobby was grinning. "Okay, I know I'm boring you. I told you not to get me started."

"No, not at all. I love seeing someone who's passionate about what they do. You don't always find that in academia. And I think I'm at the top of the list when it comes to boring in the classroom."

Alex kept quiet. She realized he was about to tell her why he was in the woods.

"I thought I was coming to see about the house today, but I found myself wanting to go to the woods. Being there was what I loved as a kid, especially this time of year. There are so many colors. It's so full of life. I found my grandfather's old still, at least a few remnants of it. I could almost hear the talking, just like the day I stumbled on them making moonshine."

Shine Bobby paused. "The psychologist is hearing voices," he added. "Now that's something." He took a sip of coffee. "They gave me the name Shine Bobby that day."

"I know," Alex said. "Your grandfather told my father you'd found the still and he gave you that name. It stuck with you for a long time."

"But you, Alex, you seem to have everything you ever wanted."

"Are you kidding?" she asked. "I'm almost broke. What about you? Don't you have everything you wished for? All you ever talked about in high school was going to college and getting your PhD."

Bobby ran his fingers through his hair. "We got what we asked for Alex, but is it enough? Isn't there more to life?"

"I don't know, Bobby. Maybe there is. I just know that every time I get a good horse I have to sell it to make ends meet. I have to sell my black colt in the January sale."

"I'm sorry things aren't going well," he sighed. "What I know for myself is that I have to make some changes in my life. I'm thinking about retiring from the University."

"Was that why you were here today, thinking about those changes?" she asked.

"Yes, I felt I needed to come back and find Shine Bobby again. I miss that kid who knew what he wanted and went after it."

CHAPTER SIX

VIOLA FLOWERS

Viola Flowers stared at the envelope in her hand and smiled. *Miss Viola Flowers,* she read. How she hated that name when she was a child. The teasing became almost unbearable when she entered school.

How could her mother do this to her? Even the name Rose would have been better. At least it was a beautiful flower. But Viola? How horrified she had been when she was told that her name was the same as those little purple things that grew at random in their yard.

But by the time Viola went to college she could see quite a different spin on her name. Viola the small and insignificant became the bold, wild thing that dared to be brave, just as the flower dared to be the first thing to stick its head above ground in spring.

Viola came into her own "flowering" as one of the children of the hippie generation. In her purple dress Viola protested the Vietnam War, and she spoke out against segregation while in her purple dress. She was one with the flower children, except she didn't use pot. She hated the smoke.

Her mother had been a chain smoker, and she had spent too many hours enduring the smoke in their car. The smoke became unbearable when they took one of their frequent trips. But those trips were always filled with something historical. History was a passion of her mother's and it became Viola's. But the smoke was still intolerable.

Little did she know that aversion would become another reason to protest when she became older. The "purple dress lady" was revived when she joined the ranks of those proponents of the anti-smoking movement. It took a lot of "Viola bravery" to do that in the nation's leading state in tobacco production.

However, in between the two purple-dress-protests times, Viola realized that she had to do something to make a living. Music seemed to be the perfect thing. She could teach and she could be a bit eccentric as musicians were allowed to be. She did, however, have to tone down a bit when she got a teaching job in a rural high school. That's where she met fellow teacher, Jane Miller, and of course along with knowing Jane came the knowing of Eva Farnsworth, a fellow card reader.

Once again she looked at the invitation in her hand. It mentioned that Robert Ferguson and Alex Jardine would also be attending the book signing and the dinner at Belle Rouge. These two were seniors at the high school when Viola first came.

Viola Flowers had directed them in their senior play and, oh, how good they were! Maybe she thought so because they were the first students she directed. For whatever reason she had kept track of them.

When Viola thought about it, it wasn't as if there were some great chasm in age between her and those first students. Viola, fresh out of college, was only four years older than those seniors she taught, and Jane Miller had only been teaching one year when Viola got to Cedarville.

Viola retired as soon as she could from teaching. Those twenty-seven years seemed to bleach her of her "purpleness." Over the years she did go through her lavender age where she dared take issue with the school's administration over certain policies. Then came her totally "white" years, drained of a desire to be a voice for the "other side." She was satisfied to simply float through the last years of teaching, moving with the current until she reached the oceanic expanse of retirement. Retirement was not an end to Viola Flowers, she thought. It was an adventure of unlimited possibilities, she tried to convince herself. But she never seemed to find those possibilities.

Of course she would accept Laurel Mackenzie's invitation. Jane had told her that Laurel's new book was ready to be released as was the movie. How thrilled they all were that Cedarville was the setting!

CHAPTER SEVEN

NEW FRIENDSHIPS BEGIN

A couple of days after Shine Bobby visited the woods, his phone rang. It was Alex. "Did you receive an invitation to a book signing followed by a dinner party at Belle Rouge?" she asked.

"I did and it sounds like fun. You received an invite, too?"

"I can't imagine why the owner of Belle Rouge would invite me," Alex said.

"Maybe she wants to get to know her neighbors. Come on, we've both been complaining that our lives are dull. This is something different and it could be fun. What if I pick you up?"

Alex hung up the phone and leaned back in the recliner. "Well, Shine Bobby, that's the closest thing to a date I've had in years. And you've certainly never asked me before."

Viola Flowers sat in her tattered lounge chair, her eyes closed. It was what she did every morning—meditate. This quiet time held such comfort for her. She felt this was the way she could get into the flow of life. And as she got older she no longer viewed life as a struggle. She had come to the realization that the circumstances of life simply needed to be accepted for what they were—happenings, with as little judgment as possible. She was not a fatalist, far from it. Life was just easier without the struggle.

When she opened her eyes she felt as if she had received a warning from her inner voice. She needed to be careful of what she might say while at the Belle Rouge dinner party. Viola didn't quite understand this feeling, but she would be aware that something out of the ordinary just might present itself.

She relaxed more deeply and let her mind search for what might lie behind the warning her intuition had given her.

Certainly she knew everyone who would be there, except Miss Mackenzie and her husband, though she did know John Miller was the sheriff, but he had already graduated from high school by the time she came. Again Viola closed her eyes and let her thoughts survey each of them.

She could see great success for Laurel Mackenzie with her writing. She also saw horses around her. When she thought on Sheriff John Miller, she saw she was about to become friends with him. All she could see around Eva and Jane was a storm. Viola didn't question any of these revelations. She moved on to her former students, Bobby and Alex.

Shine Bobby, though she didn't dare call him that to his face, was an easy person to like. He quietly went about everything he did. His grades were excellent in high school. He was thoughtful and he certainly knew what he wanted to do. Viola realized early on that Robert Ferguson would do well in academia. But somehow she wondered if he might feel he had gone as far as he could go. He had accomplished what he set out to do and he had been doing it for years.

Viola was astounded at what entered her mind next. Surely Professor Ferguson was not in a stagnant pool of his own doing.

Of all her students, she couldn't deny Alex Jardine was her favorite. Alex seemed to move through life with a calmness and a sense of purpose that amazed Viola. Now she would like to be friends with Alex, but the opportunity never arose. Alex had been successful with her horses, and she never seemed to want or need any friends.

Viola Flowers came to one conclusion as her time of meditation ended. It would be an interesting dinner.

The day before the book signing and dinner party Viola stood in front of the full length mirror and sighed. An old song from years ago popped in her head. *Shoo fly pie and apple pan dowdy.* Dowdy, that was it, the perfect word to describe the old woman who looked back at her through the mirror.

"When did I become this?" she asked herself. She had lost weight and that was good, but her wardrobe hadn't kept up with the change in her body. Faded black knit slacks, made thin by their many washings, drooped over her hips, melting in puddles around her old flip-flops. She wore no bra, only an old, equally faded black blouse. All this was covered by a wine-colored knit jacket, dotted with specks where bleach had accidentally splashed on it while it lay on the floor in the laundry room.

Viola ran her fingers through her hair, letting the salt and pepper strands fall back into place. "I had such beautiful brown hair, thick and wavy," she thought. "What happened?" she asked herself once again.

"Retirement," she answered her own question. There was no longer any reason to dress up, to keep up with the styles. Since retirement she simply languished in the stillness of her home, doing anything she damn well pleased. She read when she wanted, ate when she wanted, no school bells dictating her every movement.

Then boredom set in. She needed to get out, be with people. Last year she had signed up to substitute teach. God, how she hated it! She heard the snickers of the children. She had become the old lady who invaded their classroom, the one who demanded they be quiet, the one who constantly wore a frown, the one they all dreaded to see coming.

Viola Flowers removed her name from the following year's substitute list. The students she once knew, the ones who respected her, had moved on. No one knew her now except for a few teachers. Jane Miller was the only one with whom she ever talked.

The school had already gone through two principals since she left. She knew the present one wouldn't last much longer. Viola saw the signs. When she substituted, she had seen the young woman in her office, head in hands. She knew it just wasn't the business of school that bothered the principal. It was difficult to balance one's self between the duties of school and home. There were young children at her home, a husband who was demanding. It could tear a person apart.

Viola was lucky in that way. She didn't have to worry about a life with a husband and children. She had neither. When she saw the stress in some of her fellow teachers who had families, she wanted no part of it. But over the past year, if she allowed herself, Viola's thoughts slipped into wondering what it would be like to have children of her own, someone to take care of her in her old age.

"But just because you had children didn't mean they'd take care of you," she placated herself. She had seen that too. She had seen a lot in her almost seventy years. But she had begun to realize she probably hadn't "done" enough with her time. She hadn't "lived" enough in these past years. Viola needed to do something different, make some changes, add a little excitement in her life. She didn't know how exciting it would be, but Ms. Mackenzie's dinner party might be a start.

Viola thumbed through the phone book and dialed a number. "Yes. I'd like to make an appointment for a styling and set."

In the hours before Bobby was going to pick her up, Alex stared into her closet. "I guess these khaki slacks will be okay. The invitation did say it was an informal dinner."

She pushed the hangers back and forth. "Damn, a thrift store wouldn't even accept this stuff."

Then she spotted it, a light blue, three-quarter-length-sleeved silk blouse, hanging in the back of the closet. "Oh, I remember you," she said. "I bought you to wear in the winner's circle when

HE had the favorite in a stakes race at Churchill. That's the day I learned he had a wife in Florida. No wonder he asked me not to get my photo taken if he won the race. I guess he didn't want her to see me."

She pulled the shirt down over her head. "Might as well break you in."

Alex saw herself in the mirror. "God, what do I do with this hair? It's got a mind of its own. Hell, I'll just brush it and let it go where it wants to."

She got on her hands and knees, scattering the shoes that lay in the bottom of her closet. Then she found a forgotten pair, high heels with a low boot cut.

"Wonder if I can walk in these?" she chuckled. "Oh, hell, why not. I'll be sitting at a table most of the night. If I'm lucky Bobby will help me up and down the steps of the house."

That Robert Ferguson was ten minutes late was no surprise to Alex. Bobby moved to his own time and that was usually slow. But that ten minutes was torture for Alex. It was more time for her to look in the mirror and criticize how she looked.

But then she stopped the talk in her head and simply looked at herself. Her hair fell in natural brown waves, and women paid a lot of money to get those light streaks in their hair. Yes, they may want blond streaks where hers were gray, but it did look okay, she decided.

She concluded something else. Light blue was her color, and she did have a waist. All the work with the horses kept her body fit.

Alex heard his car rattling on the gravel drive. She peaked from behind the limp curtain to watch him, wondering, hoping that surely he wouldn't be wearing a suit.

To her horror it was worse. He was wearing khaki slacks and a light blue shirt. "Oh, God, we're dressed alike," she panicked.

There was no time to rummage through the closet again. Besides there was no other shirt to wear.

"What in the world will Bobby say when he sees what I have on?"

In the few seconds Alex had before he knocked, she began to realize that Dr. Ferguson probably wouldn't even notice.

But she was wrong. "Great minds...," he smiled when he saw her.

Viola Flowers took one final look at herself in the faded mirror of her faded car. The faded face that always looked back at her wasn't there on this evening. The foundation, rouge, eyeliner and shadow and her new hair style made the image bare some resemblance to the teacher who was about to see her former students.

Her black dress seemed to bring out the sparkle in her gray hair. Her purple shawl brought back some of the sparkle she once felt.

The door to her old Toyota creaked as she opened it. A fleeting moment of doubt crept in. "Is that who I am?" she asked herself. "A creaky old woman who no longer has a purpose except to sputter down the road of life?"

Viola Flowers did know she had one more thing she needed to DO in her life. In the forty some years she'd lived in this town, she had never gotten up the courage to even try to speak about it. There was simply no "right time" for her to do it. But the urge had been growing ever since Ms. Mackenzie invited her to this dinner party.

Viola took a deep breath and started up the sidewalk of the library. "When it's the right time, I'll do it," she vowed.

There was little time at the Cedarville Library's book signing for anyone to carry on an in-depth conversation. There were only polite hellos. Eva, Jane and Viola stood at the side of the room, seemingly engrossed in watching the people file toward the table where Laurel sat, signing their books and smiling at each person and granting their personal dedication requests. However, Viola did step away for a few minutes and become engrossed in a conversation with a woman.

When she returned Jane asked a question. "Have you two noticed how my cousin, John, hasn't moved from behind Laurel?"

"I've noticed," Eva replied. "It's as if he's always watching for something or someone."

"I guess that's what sheriffs do," Eva smiled.

Alex and Bobby headed outside after their books were signed. Alex was amazed that Laurel Mackenzie had written quite a lot in her book. She paused to read it.

"What did she write?" Bobby asked.

"Something about horses and further endeavors," Alex answered. "What do you suppose she means?"

"I think the answer will come tonight at the dinner," Bobby smiled.

CHAPTER EIGHT

NEW BEGINNINGS

Belle Rouge stood in an elegant silhouette against the orange and blue of the early evening sky. Light glowed from every window. And one couldn't help but notice that the crimson maples seemed to be swaying to the beat of some song heard only by them. If a house could be happy, this one was.

Eva and Jane left the book signing early in Jane's old Mercury, eager to welcome the dinner quests. Viola's Toyota was the next to arrive, momentarily followed by Bobby Ferguson's Civic with its dented front fender.

"Looks like we've started a used car lot," Bobby laughed. "A VERY used car lot."

Alex breathed a sigh of relief when she saw the table was set in the kitchen and not the formal dining room. She knew she would have no idea what fork or spoon to use if it were a formal setting, but she felt right at home in the kitchen.

She couldn't help but wonder if Bobby often attended formal functions connected with his professorship at the University. He surely was much more versed in such things than she. Bobby's world was far removed from hers. Her world smelled of hay, grain and sweat, both hers and her horses. She almost laughed out loud when she pictured Professor Ferguson stepping in the horse manure.

"What's so funny," Bobby asked.

"I was just imagining you back on the farm."

"Once a farmer, always a farmer," he replied.

They were standing in the kitchen when Laurel burst through the back door, closely followed by John. "What a fun time," she exclaimed. "I love these people in Cedarville. They're so kind."

Most of the time," she heard Jane whisper.

Eva introduced everyone then invited them all to sit down at the table.

"Supper is very simple," Jane said as she ladled the soup into bowls.

"And I made a green salad," Eva added. "That's about the extent of my cooking skills."

"Wait a minute," Laurel interjected. "You mean we're about to open a B and B and neither of you can cook? That second B stands for breakfast, you know."

"Viola, can you cook?" Eva asked.

"Why would you ask me?"

"We were wondering if you might like to go into business with us," Jane grinned.

"Not if I have to cook," Viola quickly added. "But I wouldn't even have to think about it if I could be useful doing something else."

"We're going to have to hire a cook," Laurel said. "Anyone have any ideas?"

It was even a surprise to herself when Alex spoke up. "I know someone. She worked in the track kitchen until her daughter was born. She can cook anything. She's from Mexico and she adds a little spice to food that makes it absolutely delicious."

"You know," Laurel smiled," I want us to remain close to the southern tradition of cooking, but I think it would be wonderful if the food were tweaked a bit."

Alex got even braver. "Her husband is a former jockey from Scotland, but he decided to stay in Kentucky when he met Maria. He couldn't make it as a jockey here because of his weight. He could ride a lot heavier in Europe, but now he just exercises horses at the track. They're having a difficult time making it financially, but if she had a job where she could bring her daughter along...."

"It's time we had a serious talk," Laurel said. "I think if we all put our heads together we could get something really special started here at Belle Rouge. Are all of you interested?"

"I know I am," Viola was the first to reply. "I'm rather tired of just sitting in my old recliner and watching."

"I sit in mine and read," Jane chimed in.

"I sit in mine and try to rest my weary bones," Alex laughed.

"I meditate in mine," Eva said.

Viola nodded in agreement.

"And I can't even find my recliner with all the clutter in my apartment," Bobby laughed.

"So how do we proceed to get everyone out of their recliners and get a business going here at Belle Rouge?" Laurel asked.

Eva offered the solution. "First we take stock of what we all can do and then we define our goals. I believe I can take care of the advertising to get people to come to Belle Rouge for a visit. I haven't done anything like that, but I know I can do it."

"I would love to decorate the house differently for every season, and I could make each room unique," said Jane, "and I love to do the table settings and, yes, I know I can't cook, but I can decorate. I'm good at organizing and keeping the books."

Viola thought for a minute. "I believe I can do tours at Belle Rouge. I love to write scripts, and the visitors would certainly love to know the history of this place."

Bobby and Alex simply stared at one another until Bobby spoke. "I don't know what either of us could add to what everyone said."

"Now it's my turn," Laurel said, "and this is where you two come in. I know what I want is very ambitious, and it may take some time, but I'm determined to do it."

"Alex," she continued. "I have a five-year-old gelding that's just standing in the field. Do you think you could bring him back to racing? He almost got there once, but we had to scratch him out of the race because of an injury. I know he can run. Do you want to give it a try?"

"I certainly do," Alex answered.

"I don't know how I could fit in," Bobby said, "but I'd love to be back here in Cedarville, doing something with the land and working with Alex. My light schedule at the university would allow me to do that every afternoon and on the weekends. Could you use my help, Alex?"

"Oh, Bobby, I certainly could use the help."

Laurel leaned forward in her excitement. "As we've been talking, an idea has formed in my head. We have a cook in mind, and the B and B seems well on its way. And I'll tell you this, I'm going to add more horses to my racing stable. Bobby, you have a house next door. What if it were fixed up and it could become the home of Maria and her family. With more horses added, say, yearlings and two-year-olds, we'll need someone to break them. Maria's husband could be hired to handle the young horses."

Now Alex became even more energized. "We could keep the broodmares on my farm...." Then she took a deep breath. "But my fields are so over grazed I don't know...."

"Why don't I fence my place in," this time it was Bobby who became excited. "The land has been fallow for years and the grass is plentiful. I noticed that when I went to the woods the other day."

John Miller spoke for the first time. "My cousin still operates the family construction company. I don't think it would take too much to make your house livable for...what's the exercise boy's name?"

Alex answered. "We call him Cal, but his last name is MacCallum."

"Oh, my god," Laurel gasped. That's the name of Mrs. Lennox's horse trainer."

"I haven't read your book yet, Laurel. Who's Mrs. Lennox?" Alex asked.

Laurel's voice was shaking. "She's a friend of the Kilgores, the people who built Belle Rouge. Please don't tell me we're going back into the past again."

"Maybe we're simply tying the past to the present," Viola whispered.

CHAPTER NINE

NEW ALLIES

When Viola got home she dropped her car keys in the basket by the door as usual and plopped herself down in the recliner. "Old friend," she grinned, "I don't think I'll be seeing you as much as usual in the near future."

As she pondered the happenings that had taken place in the last few hours, her thoughts turned to Jane. She had heard Jane's response when Laurel said the people in Cedarville were kind.

Jane had been a close friend while they were teaching. But close friends at work seldom turned into socializing after work, at least it didn't happen for them. However, Jane had confided some personal things when they often had free periods at the same time or when they both lingered after school.

Viola knew Jane had been terribly hurt by a man, and Viola even suspected that a child had been involved. Jane never specifically mentioned a child, but it was the way she looked at times when she was with certain students. It was almost if they reminded her of someone, because they all had something in common—dark hair and blue eyes.

Viola knew she should have kept up with Jane more than she had, and now, since they would be working together at Belle Rouge, she could do that.

Jane had shared with Viola some of the problems her good friend Eva Farnsworth had. Her husband had deserted her and left with a much younger woman. That had to be so humiliating for her. Eva had problems making ends meet, but she did get some alimony and had worked in a local store which gave her some Social Security for her retirement.

Still it had to be difficult for her. But after watching Eva at the dinner, Viola knew this woman would always find some joy in whatever life brought. Viola also realized she could learn a few things from Eva. Where Eva's thoughts found the joy, Viola's thoughts often turned to the sadness of her long-held secret.

She did see a lot of happiness for Alex and Bobby. They should have been together a long time ago, but their pathways took them away from each other. It would be different now. However, Viola could see something dark ahead of them. She would not allow herself to look any farther. They both needed to enjoy each other, at least for a while.

Viola had taken an instant liking to Laurel Mackenzie. Laurel was going to be a catalyst for a lot of changes in everyone's life. That was both exciting and a bit scary.

John Miller was an interesting person. He'd been quiet most of the evening, but Viola knew he was taking in all the conversation. He was sizing up the situation especially with the three new people who sat at the dinner table. It was easy for Viola to see that he grounded Laurel. Sheriff Miller was very logical and, in his own way, an intuitive. Perhaps it came from his experience in law enforcement and not from the ethers, as Viola's did.

He had done a curious thing when Viola headed for her car after dinner. He followed her, opened the door for her, leaned in the window and almost whispered. "May I come by your house early tomorrow morning before I go to work?"

She had agreed, of course, but now with that on her mind, she couldn't go to sleep. She picked up Laurel's book and began to read.

Bobby Ferguson had been so deep in thought when they left Belle Rouge that he forgot to open Alex's car door for her, but she didn't seem to notice. She wasn't used to anyone doing something like that for her anyway.

The heater of the car didn't have time to warm up by the time they pulled into Alex's driveway. Bobby never turned off the ignition, but they sat there for a few minutes, neither one knowing why they didn't move.

Finally, Bobby spoke. "Is it okay if I come by tomorrow?"

"Sure," Alex replied. "Come anytime you want."

Bobby Ferguson's brain was too tired to think, to analyze, as it usually did. He just drove as if he and the car were on automatic, honing in on the familiarity of his dark and dreary apartment.

He parked the car in front of the apartment building, stumbled up the steps and managed to unlock the door. He wondered why his brain didn't seem to be working as he took off his pants and shirt, letting them fall to the floor. Exhausted, he fell into bed and pulled the covers over him, falling asleep immediately. But his brain was not as dead. The activity had simply moved into a different place. Shine Bobby was about to have a vivid dream about Alex.

Alex was tired, but she realized she was happier than she had been in a long while. Laurel Mackenzie had breathed new life into everyone who had been at the dinner party. And it was so good to reconnect with Bobby and now he had asked to come by.

As she dropped into bed she couldn't help but wonder why she and Bobby seemed to click now. They certainly hadn't in high school. He was simply the brainy guy who lived next door. "Life is funny," she said as she fell into a restful sleep.

Viola sat with her morning coffee and watched the sun come up. She only had a couple hours sleep because she couldn't put Laurel's book down. While reading she had come to the conclusion that the words held more truth than fiction.

A knock at the door jolted her from her thoughts. "Come in," she invited the sheriff into the living room. "How about a cup of coffee?" she asked.

"I'd like that," he replied as he wearily sank into the cushions of the sofa.

Viola handed him the cup. "You take it black. Don't you," she stated rather than asked.

John Miller smiled. "I guess you're wondering why I wanted to talk to you, and I'm not really sure why I need to. I think I just need to share a few things with someone who wasn't caught up in everything that happened after Laurel bought Belle Rouge."

"You can trust me, John. I can tell something is bothering you and I have read the book and I know a lot of it is truth."

John stared into the coffee cup. "All of it," he replied. "We all thought Laurel was losing her mind. She saw people in the house. She saw what they did to each other. Then there was Lucien Caulder. What a piece of work he was."

"I'm just curious," Viola said, "what happened to Belle Rouge after Sumner and Claire Kilgore died."

"Sheriff Miller, Alexandra Lennox and the Prices, Laurel's ancestors who adopted Claire's child, took care of Belle Rouge for a while. Mr. and Mrs. Price never wanted to live in the house and raise the child there. When they decided to move to North Carolina, the place was sold in two parcels. A family from Louisville who knew Alexandra bought the land where the house sits to use as a summer house. They seldom came but they did keep the place up. The Ferguson family bought the other parcel and some years later they sold part of theirs to the Jardine family. Laurel bought the house and its land three years ago from the descendants of the original buyer."

"John, does it feel to you as if there is another gathering of the ghosts around Belle Rouge? Are you afraid Laurel may be drawn in again?"

"I don't know, but I feel better with you, Bobby and Alex involved with the B and B and the addition of horses. Laurel is so thrilled that her dream of owning a thoroughbred farm and racing the horses is finally coming about. I hope that will occupy her mind and not let her be drawn back into all this weird stuff."

"But something else is bothering you. What is it John?"

"Laurel doesn't know about this yet, but I've been contacted by her publisher, offering me a job as head of security when she goes on tour promoting the book."

"Isn't that a bit strange to find it necessary to have a security detail for a book tour?" Viola asked.

"They've gotten word that a radical religious group is going to protest wherever she appears. They're claiming that she's some sort of a heretic for writing about this sort of stuff. They've called her…"

"A witch," Viola sighed.

After John left Viola was exhausted, but when she lay down on her bed she couldn't quiet her mind. She went to the medicine cabinet and took out a bottle of sleeping pills. "I don't think one is enough," she said.

CHAPTER TEN

OLD ACQUAINTANCE

Bobby Ferguson was still in heavy sleep when the phone jangled him awake. "Sure, Alex, I'll be there in about thirty minutes. I don't have any classes this morning. See you at the hospital."

He threw on the same clothes he'd had on the previous night. He ran to the bathroom, splashed water on his face and brushed his hair, while he swished the mouthwash around in his mouth.

He was thankful he had an extra jacket in the car because he'd forgotten to grab one on his way out of the apartment. The heater of the car was just warming up as he pulled onto the interstate. He was also beginning to remember his dream about Alex. "Get a grip. Now is not the time for that."

The doctor sought out Alex in the hospital waiting room. "A neighbor found her," he said. "They usually have coffee together in the mornings and, when Miss Flowers didn't answer her knock, she began to look through each window. She could see her lying on the bedroom floor and called 911."

"Has she had a stroke?" Alex asked.

"No," the nurse replied. "We believe she stumbled on a bath mat when she came out of the bathroom and hit her head on a table. There was an open bottle of sleeping pills on the floor beside her. You can imagine—the blow to her head knocked her unconscious and then the sleeping pills kept her from waking up."

"Thank God the neighbor found her," Alex said.

She spotted Bobby's car pulling into the parking lot and rushed to meet him.

"Is she okay?" he asked.

"Viola's sleeping and it might be a while before she wakes up. Can you stay?"

"Of course," he replied. "How did you get word of what happened?"

"According to the doctor there was a piece of paper with my name and phone number on the table where she hit her head."

An hour had passed when Alex woke with a start, realizing her head was resting on Bobby Ferguson's shoulder. "Sorry," she murmured.

He grinned. "You've had a stressful morning. It's normal to need rest after a shock like this."

Alex stretched and yawned. "Is this the psychologist speaking?"

Before he could answer, Alex sat bolt upright. "I haven't fed the horses this morning. Bobby, could you hold fort here? I'll be back within an hour."

"Yes," he assured her. "Take your time. Viola won't wake up for a while. I think I'll go next door and get something to eat. I'll tell the lady at the desk where to find me if she needs me."

Twenty minutes later he returned to notice the receptionist hanging up the phone. "I was getting ready to phone you. Miss Flowers is awake and is asking for you."

"Are you sure it's for me and not Miss Jardine?"

"I'm sure," she replied. "Go down that hall," she pointed. "The nurse will show you to her room."

Bobby had no clue as to what to expect when he entered Viola's room, though he did have a question. How did she even know he had come to the hospital? "Oh, yes," he smiled. "She does see into the future." But unknowingly to Bobby Ferguson, Viola Flowers also knew a secret from the past—her past.

Bobby listened while Viola related a story. When she had finished Bobby patted her hand. When she dozed off again he went to the waiting room.

Still stunned from his conversation with Viola, he plopped down in a chair. He would honor Miss Flowers' request. He wouldn't reveal the content of their conversation, but Professor Ferguson knew that it wouldn't be long before Viola would have to do so.

Alex had tried not to soil her clothes as she dumped the feed into the tubs for her horses. However, she had forgotten to change her shoes. Now she had to make a hurried stop at the house to change into some clean ones. The quickest thing she could do was slip into the ones that she wore to the dinner last evening. They were still by her recliner where she had left them.

Bobby heard the click of her heels when she came across the waiting room toward him. How his heart went out to her. How he hoped he could help her with what was to come. A seed was planted at the very moment she sat down next to him. Shine Bobby was going to fall in love.

"Have you had any news about Viola?" Alex asked.

"She'll be ready to go in about an hour," he replied. "But she can't be left alone in her house, at least for a few days."

"We'll take her to my house," she assured him. "She can have the downstairs bedroom and my couch makes a bed and I'll sleep there so I can hear her if she needs something. Bobby," she continued, "can you spend some time with us?"

He reached over and took her hand. "Of course I will."

Sheriff Miller had been in his office for a couple of hours when the phone rang. It was the EMS worker who was first on the scene at Viola Flowers' house. After the worker told him what happened, he exclaimed. "You found what?" the sheriff asked. .... "Is it still in the house?" .... "No, don't tell anyone. I'll check it out."

He grabbed his car keys and called back to his secretary. "I'll be on my cell phone if you need me."

When he got to Viola's driveway he dialed a phone number. "Jane, what did you do with the fetish you found when you fell down your steps a couple of years ago? I thought it burned up in Lucien's house."

CHAPTER ELEVEN

A PARTY OF THREE

Things had happened so quickly in the hours since Laurel's dinner party. It was time to pause and take a deep breath. That's exactly what Viola Flowers did as she nestled into the soft down on Alex Jardine's bed. She had argued that she could sleep on Alex's sofa bed, but to no avail. Alex insisted she take the bedroom.

Viola had an uneasy feeling from the moment she began reading Laurel's book, but here in Alex's house she felt safe. Alex was close by and Bobby Ferguson was going to stay with them when he was not at the university.

She couldn't remember all of what happened to her that morning. She remembered not being able to go back to sleep after John Miller's visit. She knew she went to the bathroom and she remembered taking two sleeping pills. She remembered seeing something on the table beside the bed. Though she tried she couldn't remember exactly what it was.

Then she felt the hair raise up on the back of her neck. If something she didn't recognize was there on her table, someone had to have been in her house that night while she had been reading in the living room. They didn't intend to rob her; in fact, it was just the opposite. They left something for her. There was danger around. She could feel it.

But right at this moment, she assured herself, she was safe with Alex and Bobby. But once again she felt the cold chill. Did the secret she was harboring have anything to do with all this? Had she put Bobby in danger by confiding in him?

That evening Viola fell asleep lulled by the sound of Alex and Bobby talking in the living room. She heard Bobby say goodnight. Then she heard his footsteps going up the stairs. Alex was humming. Then the light in the living room went out. "Wonder when there will be two pair of footsteps going to the upstairs bedroom," she remembered thinking as she fell into a restful sleep.

A couple of days later, before daylight, Alex left for the barn. She needed no flashlight for the moon was bright in the December sky. She slid back the barn door and heard a soft nicker that was soon echoing from stall to stall.

"Don't be so impatient," she said. She had laid out each bucket the night before so all she had to do was dump the grain into each feed box. When she was finished she stopped in the runway listening to the crunching of her contented horses. She took a deep breath and inhaled the aroma of the sweet feed. This was her world. This was where she belonged.

Alex flicked on the light in the office and grabbed a clean horse blanket from its hook on the wall, wrapped it around her and headed for the old recliner in the corner.

The sleeper sofa on which she had been sleeping since Viola came was not kind to her body. It only accentuated the aching. But the old chair offered some relief. She cuddled into the warmth of the blanket and began to reflect.

She was used to being alone, but since the track had closed for the winter she had little contact of the human kind. She missed having someone with whom to talk. When the track was open her routine had been the camaraderie at the track followed by the silence in her house. Somehow it seemed to balance out her life. But things had changed since the dinner party. Now there were distinct voices in her house, both Viola's and Shine Bobby's. It was so different from the silence, having their voices there, and she liked it.

Bobby first realized he was cold. Automatically he reached for a quilt at the foot of the bed. Then he remembered that he wasn't in his bed. He was upstairs in Alex's house. Under the covers he was realizing that he preferred to be in Alex's bed with Alex in it.

"Calm down, old boy," he chuckled. No one would guess that the rumpled old psychology professor would have such cravings. No one would guess how he sometime settled his libido. There was a certain female "acquaintance" that would do so for a bit of money. He wasn't proud of what he did, but it was always better, he told himself, to relate to a woman who meant nothing to him except the gratification she provided. He had always been careful to use protection. No need for the embarrassment of telling a doctor how he got a rash.

Hastily, Bobby drew the covers tightly around him. The thought of being with someone he knew and liked sent a chill up his spine. He knew what the psychologist in him would do if it were dealing with someone else. He would try to get to the root of the problem of the patient's fear of commitment, the fear of intimacy, the fear of responsibility, the fear of a relationship if one couldn't measure up to expectations, the fear of the fear of the fear. Perhaps that word should be capitalized. FEAR.

Alex told herself she was insisting on Viola's staying in her house for Viola's protection, but truthfully she knew if Viola went home Bobby might too.

They quite easily had fallen into a routine. Viola would be the first to admit she loved the thought of someone looking out for her. Gone, at least for a while, was her secret fear that she would die alone and no one would find her for days.

She and Alex were enjoying each other's company. Their afternoon talks had become a daily routine, and there was something else in which she was finding joy. Alex would excuse herself in time to cook supper for Bobby's return. Viola knew Alex had never felt she might enjoy cooking, she was such an outdoor person, but actually she had prepared some tasty casseroles and pot roasts.

It was also lovely for Viola to watch how Bobby and Alex interacted with each other when he came through the door in the afternoon. Viola knew it wouldn't be long before Alex would leave the lumpy sofa bed and tiptoe upstairs to join Bobby. "Tonight would be a good time," she thought. She would go to her bedroom a bit early, stating her desire to read her new book Bobby bought for her.

Her plan worked. An hour after Viola turned in she heard the creak of the stairs. When she peeked through the crack in her bedroom door, Alex was nowhere to be found.

Sheriff Miller had several long talks with his cousin, but Jane kept insisting she never saw the fetish after she left it at Lucien's. She assumed it burned up in the house fire.

"Who could have retrieved it?" Miller asked. Neither of them had a logical answer.

After finding it at Viola's, the sheriff vowed no one would have access to this evil thing again. However, he couldn't burn it. It was evidence at what might turn out to be a crime scene at Viola Flowers' house. He placed it in the evidence room at the court house, appropriately marking it.

He was making his way back toward his office when he happened to glance out the glass door. He saw a woman exit her car and head toward the County Court Clerk's office across the street. His eye for detail kicked in.

The woman was tall, thin and her black curly hair loosely hung to her shoulders. He felt as if he'd seen her before. Then he noticed the license plate on her car. Arkansas. He certainly didn't have any acquaintances in that state. Still, he decided, he would talk to someone in the clerk's office after lunch. Perhaps his chief deputy's wife would be a good choice.

Bobby drove Viola to Belle Rouge on his way to the university. "I want to ask you something," he said. "This is my thirty-first year of teaching. I'm thinking of turning in my resignation at the Fall break. Does that sound crazy to you?"

"More importantly, Bobby, does it feel right for you?"

"I'm just so tired of the routine, Viola. When I step into that classroom…."

"You love it here on the farm. Don't you? And you love being with Alex," she smiled.

"Is it that noticeable?" he asked.

"Follow your heart, Bobby." Viola answered.

CHAPTER TWELVE

A STRANGER IN TOWN

Sheriff Miller made his way to the County Clerk's office as he returned from lunch. He headed toward the back room where he found his deputy's wife at her desk. "Hi there," he greeted her. "Would you happen to have spoken to the woman who came in here about eleven this morning? She was tall, thin, black hair...."

"Yes," she answered. "She'd be hard to forget."

"Do you know what she was doing here?"

"She was looking in the wills and the death certificates. She thought she might have some relatives in this area."

"Thanks," he called back at her as he started to leave.

"Oh, Sheriff...this isn't the first time she's been here. She was here at the time of Laurel's book signing. She said she was going there to get her book signed."

"That's where I've seen her," he assured himself. "Viola was talking to her."

When he got back to his office, Sheriff Miller called Viola. "How are you feeling?" he asked. "That's great .... Viola do you recall talking to a woman at the book signing? I thought I saw you talking to someone I didn't know .... What? .... You told her you were a clairvoyant? Why would you say that to a stranger? .... Oh, she just seemed to have a way about her that made talking to her very easy," he repeated.

John Miller hung up the phone and reared back in his chair. "I don't like this a bit. I have a feeling. But surely it can't be true."

Again he picked up the phone. "Hi, Honey. I was just wondering if you remember signing a book that night for a tall,

thin woman with black hair. She wasn't from around here." ....
"You do? Did you happen to remember her name? Arianna
Hull," he repeated .... "No, no, nothing's wrong. I just saw her
this morning at the courthouse, and I was trying to place where
I'd seen her before? .... What?" he lunged forward. "She's
signed up to be your first guest next week at Belle Rouge?"

When he hung up the phone the sheriff called to his
secretary. "Will you ask Mike to come in, please?"

In a few moments the chief deputy entered the office. "What
can I do for you, Boss?" he asked.

"Are you and your wife going to the lake in Hot Springs next
week?"

"Sure are," the deputy replied.

"You're studying to be a detective, right? How about taking
on your first case."

"Love it," Mike answered.

Sheriff Miller wrote down a name and handed it to the
deputy. "See what you can find out about this Arianna Hull and
her family. Give me a call the minute you learn anything."

In the muted moonlight that came through the bedroom
window, Bobby Ferguson watched Alex undress. Her hair was
growing longer, he noticed. It flattered her. He liked her
muscular body, the way the muscles in her back rippled as she
moved her arms.

Alex, naked, slipped into the warm spot offered her next to
him. She couldn't help but think that Bobby seemed to know a
lot about the act of sexual arousal, but she certainly wasn't going
to ask him how he knew so much. If she did, he might ask her
about her past affairs and that was something she wanted to keep
to herself.

The next day at lunch Alex asked Bobby, "Do you think
Viola is well enough to be driving?"

"I think she'd do it even if we tried to stop her," he grinned. "Besides, she's really looking forward to working at Belle Rouge when it opens next week as a B and B."

"I do think she's getting tired of staying here," Alex said.

"From what she infers to me she's not too anxious to go back to her house."

"She doesn't own the place, Bobby. She's been renting all these years."

"I thought at one time we could move her into the house on my place, but your friends Cal and Maria will be coming next week."

"I guess we'll just have to wait and see what plays out," Alex sighed.

Bobby reached over and took her hand. "I think you're right," he grinned.

CHAPTER THIRTEEN

TRAGEDY STRIKES

Jane and Viola had been at Belle Rouge for an hour before Jane said, "It's not like Eva to be this late. I've tried calling her but her phone goes to voice mail."

"I have a feeling we may need to check on her," Viola said.

When the two women pulled into Eva's driveway, her car was still there. Jane went ahead and knocked on the door. When there was no answer she tried the doorknob and it opened. Eva was sitting in a chair in the living room, still in her robe.

"Oh, my god," she cried out.

Viola pushed her way past Jane. "I'll call 911. You call John," she ordered.

John arrived just as the stretcher was being carried out of the house. He could see Eva was hardly breathing. When the ambulance turned on its siren and headed toward the hospital, John gave an order. "Get in my car," he told the bewildered women.

"You go with John, Viola. I'll follow in my car."

The sheriff turned on his siren as Viola asked, "What's going on John? First me and now Eva."

"Viola, I'm not sure we got to Eva in time. Jane is really going to need you. Eva was her best friend."

"I understand," she whispered.

They had been at the hospital for thirty minutes before John told Viola that he was going to take his cousin to get some coffee. Seconds later a woman in a doctor's coat approached Viola.

"Are you with Eva Farnsworth?" she asked.

When Viola nodded, the doctor continued. "I'm so sorry," she said. "Mrs. Farnsworth didn't survive the stroke."

Viola collapsed in a chair. "Poor Jane."

"Miss Flowers, please give both Miss Miller and Laurel Mackenzie a message. Tell them that dreams and desires must go forward. They now have another guardian angel to assist them."

Viola hardly noticed as the tall doctor with the Jamaican accent seemed to glide down the hall. She came to herself when she saw Laurel coming from the opposite direction.

Laurel stopped in her tracks as she caught a glimpse of the doctor disappearing around the corner. "Viola," she cried. "What's Nila doing here?"

Obviously shaken, Laurel collapsed into the closest chair. Viola sat down beside her, taking her hand. "What is it?" she asked.

Laurel's voice was shaking. "That doctor is the one who lived with Jane's cousin in Savannah."

"Oh," Viola sighed. "Yes, she's the doctor who appeared to you a year after her death in a plane crash. She helped you solve some of the problems you found at Belle Rouge."

"What's she doing here, Viola?"

"I believe she's here to help us through this very difficult time."

CHAPTER FOURTEEN

THE PRODIGAL DAUGHTER

It was late in the afternoon when they all gathered around the kitchen table at Belle Rouge. Laurel was the first to speak. "I don't know exactly what's happening, but Nila was there at the hospital when Eva died. She gave Viola a message that we needed to move forward with our dreams and desires. And she said we now had another guardian angel with us."

Jane stifled a sob.

"I don't know what's coming. I just know we need to be brave," Laurel continued.

"And we need to be on alert," John added. "Laurel and I will be leaving soon on the book tour. Her publisher requested two security people, but I've asked him to allow one to be stationed here at Belle Rouge. I can take care of Laurel We'll both feel more comfortable if one of my deputies is hired as the security guard here on the farm. I know you'll feel safer with him around."

The sheriff turned to Alex and Bobby. "Will you two keep an eye out for Jane and Viola too?"

"Of course we will," Bobby replied.

"Alex," John asked, "do you trust Cal and Maria?"

"Yes, I do." she answered.

Laurel stood up. "The funeral is day after tomorrow. Let's don't do anything else but remember Eva till then and what a dear she was to all of us. But," she looked at each one of them. "Can we continue as planned with getting the house ready for the opening next week?"

Jane wiped her eyes. "That's what Eva would have wanted."

Viola lingered behind to speak to John. "Was Eva's death a natural cause? No fetish?"

"No fetish. That dammed thing is safely locked up in the evidence room at the court house. But," he continued, "Eva had this look on her face. It was almost as if she were frightened to death. But please don't tell anyone else. I don't want to alarm them."

The chapel was filled with people, some having to stand in the back. Jane sat in the front row, flanked by John and Laurel. Bobby, Viola and Alex sat just behind them. It was doubtful any of them heard much of the minister's words, only snippets now and again. "Friend...kind...dedicated...missed."

Through the entire service Jane sat, stoic, staring ahead, detached. It was only when the service was over and she started to stand that she faltered. John grabbed one arm while Laurel latched on to the other as they followed the casket toward the door. Bobby, Alex and Viola fell in behind them.

Bobby noticed that Laurel paused near the back row of the chapel. It was only when she moved on that Bobby recognized a woman sitting in the pew. She seemed surprised when she saw him. Bobby knew he was blushing. He only hoped Alex hadn't noticed. However, he knew Viola never seemed to miss anything.

Viola spent the night at Jane's house, hoping Jane would want to spend the evening talking about Eva. But that was not to be. The next morning as they got ready to leave for Belle Rouge, Jane seemed to move about like a robot. She knew she shouldn't rush her into talking. Giving her time was the only thing Viola could do.

When they arrived at Belle Rouge, John and Laurel were just finishing their breakfast. Simultaneously they looked to Viola who shook her head and mimed the word "no."

"My agent," Laurel spoke, "wants me to get a physical. Guess they don't want a lawsuit if I get sick on this book tour. At least they didn't ask for a psych exam. Don't know if I could pass that one," she laughed.

"Did you invite Beth back to the house after the service?" John asked. "I saw her at the chapel."

"I tried to find her after the interment, but she'd gone."

"Your daughter's a strange one, Laurel."

"I know, John. I thought we'd gotten things straightened out when all this weird stuff at Belle Rouge was over. She told me she was going to enroll at the University in Louisville for a higher degree, and I assumed we could spend more time together. I tried, but she said she needed time to adjust at the university. We did speak on the phone at least once a week. She said she was going to her father's that Christmas. She called when she came back to start her second semester and asked if we could have lunch. I was thrilled, but we actually just had some small talk. There was no explanation as to what was going on in her life. I know not to push Beth or she would pull away even more. I just decided to let her take the lead."

"Doesn't she graduate with her master's this Spring?" John asked. "What's she going to do then?"

"I have no idea. She may tell me. But I know I have to let her initiate the conversation."

Viola listened intently to the conversation. "So that's who Laurel spoke to at the back of the chapel. It was easy to see that Bobby knew her. Was she a student of his?"

Laurel broke into Viola's thoughts. "I'd better get going for my doctor's appointment."

After Laurel left, John rose from the table. When he saw Viola's quizzical look he said, "They have a complicated relationship. Beth blames her mother for the divorce from her father."

Jane had wandered off into the parlor. She sat with her back to the doorway, staring into the dimly burning log in the fireplace. The flame sputtered as part of the log fell apart. Then as if fueled by some invisible source, the flame grew, licking its way up the chimney.

Jane shivered as a chill seemed to pass through her. "I know you're here, Eva," she whispered. Just then a small picture frame fell from an end table across the room. When Jane picked up the broken frame, she saw it was a photo of Laurel and Beth.

"It's beginning," she thought.

CHAPTER FIFTEEN

JANE

Like some gray, foreboding cloud, a nagging thought had hung over Jane from the moment she realized she was pregnant. What would her grandmother do when she told her? But there was no one else she could turn to for help. She couldn't turn to Lucien Caulder for help. She knew in her heart that he would never marry her. Lucien was not the sort of young man who would take to settling down, and besides, she had a powerful drive to get her college degree.

Jane always smiled when she thought of her grandmother, bold, straight forward, and the only one in the family whom Jane could turn to in times of trouble. True, there had only been a handful of times, childish things. But now she would have to drop out of college because she was pregnant. Would her grandmother once again stand by her?

Certainly her mother wouldn't. What other people thought meant more to her mother than anything concerning her only child, a daughter she never wanted. Her mother's only desire was for a boy, and she made that quite clear. Sometimes Jane wished she could trade places with her cousin John. His parents were perfect in Jane's eyes.

Jane's father offered no consolation to her. He only followed the direction her mother gave him. She could not believe he was the son of her grandmother. Why couldn't he be more like her.

Her grandmother had tried to intervene when her mother lashed out at her, but it only intensified her mother's anger. It was her mother's decision that Jane should go to Savannah and live with a cousin during her pregnancy. Her cousin's friend would see to the adoption.

The hate Jane felt for her mother was indescribable. She didn't dare display it, so she stuffed it down deep inside her where it remained. The anger only intensified when her father was killed shortly after she returned from Savannah. Some said it was an accident, how the team of horses must have spooked over something while her father was plowing the back field. He fell beneath the disc. There was no open casket.

She never believed her father's death was an accident. She knew he did it on purpose. Her mother had driven him to it.

Jane would never forget the week after the funeral when her grandmother took some drastic actions. She had asked Jane and her mother to join her in the kitchen. There was an envelope laying on the kitchen table just within her grandmother's reach.

For what seemed like an eternity, her grandmother stared at her mother, her gaze never wavering, her jaw set like some steel trap. Then her grandmother began.

"I have watched as you emasculated my son, driving him to his grave. I have watched you manifest your jealous rage against my granddaughter. I cannot even begin to tell you how much I despise you, especially for how easily you saw to it that Jane's baby would never become a part of my family. I believe you have successfully ended any chance of this family's continuing its lineage."

Jane could see her mother begin to shrink. But her grandmother was not yet finished. "You are no longer welcome in this house, my house. You will leave in two days. In this envelope is a railway ticket back to your people in Tennessee. The money enclosed will see you through for about a year. Then you will have to figure out how you will survive after that. Perhaps your family is more kind than you. Or perhaps some unlucky man will come into your life and you can once again bleed the very life out of him."

Her grandmother clenched the envelope and shoved it into her mother's hand. Her mother was gone in the allotted time. She and her grandmother stood together on the front porch where they could see the train as it pulled out of the station. Simultaneously they took a deep breath. They both knew a terrible time in their life had just ended.

CHAPTER SIXTEEN

THE PAST RETURNS

Jane asked Viola if she would consider moving in with her. It was during one of their evening talks that Jane finally began to open up.

"Viola, why has the fetish appeared again? And now Laurel says she saw Nila at the hospital. And Barney's descendant, Mr. MacCallum, has come into our lives." Tears began to fill Jane's eyes. "Why did Eva have to die?" She took a deep breath. "Is there really something to this thing about guardian angels?"

"I think it's possible," Viola said.

Jane's voice began to quaver. "Is something so terrible about to happen that Eva thought she could protect us more by becoming another of our angels like Nila and Barney?"

It was difficult for Viola to sleep during the nights that followed. Her mind kept racing, trying to find answers to Jane's questions. But she could find none. "Only time held those answers," she concluded.

Viola was happy John Miller felt safe in sharing information with her, but sometimes what he said was a bit overwhelming. The fetish he found in her bedroom was the same one that had been used by Genevieve, Sumner Kilgore's mulatto mistress. Lucien Caulder, her descendant, possessed it at one time. The fetish was in Jane's house when she fell some years back. Then Jane had placed it in Lucien's house just before it burned.

"So, how did it survive the fire and who placed it in my house?" Viola had asked the sheriff. "And why?"

Sheriff Miller just shook his head. "There's something else." Then he related that a strange woman was in town looking for her ancestors and she was scheduled to be one of the first guests when Belle Rouge opened as a B and B. Somehow, she's connected to all this."

Viola knew she would have to be vigilant in the coming days. Lenny, the deputy, would be staying at Belle Rouge and that was comforting.

She would have liked to confide in Bobby and Alex, but she'd promised the sheriff she would tell no one about the content of their conversations.

Viola had many questions. Again she asked, "Why me? Why did he confide in me and not Bobby? It seems to me Bobby would be the logical one."

She was sure the sheriff knew what he was doing. She was simply going to have to trust him. And she knew she would be the one who would have to look after Jane. "Life is so filled with unexpected things," she said to herself.

The activity at Belle Rouge was in a hectic state. Lenny moved into a guest studio apartment Laurel had built at the barn. Cal and Maria were in the process of moving into the Ferguson cottage, and Alex secured a couple of stalls at Churchill Downs. She moved Laurel's gelding there in order to re-start his training.

It was Bobby who was troubling to Viola. He seemed to be worried. Viola knew it must have something to do with Laurel's daughter. She had seen the alarm on his face when he saw her at the funeral.

Alex also recognized that Bobby had been different since Eva's funeral. He was quiet and withdrawn. He didn't know Eva that well, so it couldn't be about her. Something else had to be bothering him.

When his cell phone rang the day after the funeral, Alex saw him glance at the number, then hurry outside to take the call. She peeped through the window. She could tell he was agitated.

When he came inside he didn't make eye contact. He simply picked up his keys and headed for the door. "I have to take care of something at the university," he called back to her.

Alex felt as if she had hit her in the pit of her stomach. It was the same feeling she had years ago when she found out her lover was married. She then did what she always did when she felt something was terribly wrong. She ran to the barn, picked up a pitchfork and began to clean the stalls. "Keep busy, keep busy," she repeated again and again.

The phone in Alex's office rang. It was Laurel. "Yes, I can have lunch with you" .... "No, Bobby had to go to the university" .... "I'll see you in half an hour."

When they were gathered in the kitchen at Belle Rouge, John handed each of them a piece of paper. "Here's our schedule for the book tour," he said. "Two stops in Nashville, one just south of there in Franklin. Two stops in Atlanta, two in Savannah."

Viola noticed that Jane shuttered when he mentioned Savannah. She remembered the part in Laurel's book that dealt with that city. From what Eva told her she also knew that's where Jane had given up her child that was fathered by Lucien Caulder.

John continued. "From Savannah we go to Charlestown, then up to Ashville, over to Knoxville and finally Chattanooga before we arrive back here a week before Christmas."

Viola noticed something else. Laurel wasn't paying attention to anything John was saying. She simply sat at the table and grinned.

When John finished she said, "I have an announcement. You all know I went to the doctor this morning for my physical."

Unexpectedly John reached over and took her hand. "Something's not wrong. Is it?"

Her smile grew wider. "I really don't quite know how to answer that, so I'll just say it. This forty something year old person is unbelievably—pregnant."

John jumped to his feet. "Oh, my god. Oh, my god," was all he managed.

"I take it that's a happy dance," Laurel said.

He pulled her to her feet and twirled her around. He put his hands on her shoulders and looked her squarely in the eyes. "I love you, Laurel Mackenzie Miller."

"Now that's something for a man who seldom shows his emotions," she responded. "Come on, sit down. I want to say something else."

"Churchill Downs' November meet is going on, so, Alex, I want you to take this check and claim a couple of horses."

"Oh, my," Alex almost shouted. "This much money? Are you sure?"

"If you have some money left, go to the horse sale in Lexington and get us a couple of babies. And I'm wondering if you'd like to sell half-interest in your black colt."

"Bobby's interested in going in on him. I'll have to talk with him—when I see him," Alex responded.

Now Viola was certain something had happened between Alex and Bobby. When she glanced at Sheriff Miller, she was sure he felt the same thing.

Laurel was still speaking. "Alex, I know you haven't made plans as to which stallions you want to breed to your mares. For part-interest in the foals, I'll pay the stud fees. I know some of those fees are terribly high, but let's stay at ten thousand and under."

When Alex caught her breath she said, "I can do that. I have a couple of stallions in mind. Do you have time to go see them?"

"No, no," Laurel answered. "I trust your judgment entirely. When we return in a few weeks, I just want to see some new horses at Belle Rouge and at Churchill Downs. And Alex, would you mind picking up my racing silks at the shop. They'll be ready tomorrow."

"If the horses we claim are in good shape, I'll try to have them ready to run at Turfway in December. Laurel, I simply can't believe this."

On her way home Alex stopped at the Ferguson place when she saw Cal and Maria carrying some boxes into the house.

The old clapboard had been replaced by a beige vinyl siding. Red shutters framed windows which were trimmed in white. "The outside changes were amazing," Alex thought. But the changes inside were even more striking. Vinyl flooring had been laid in the kitchen which also had new white appliances. New carpeting graced the living room and the two bedrooms. The upstairs had not been redone, but it could hold a good amount of storage.

Alex stepped back onto the front porch just as Cal was coming in with another load. "The house is beautiful," he said in his soft Scottish accent. "I could never have imagined its looking this good. I am just so thankful. I have never lived in such a house since I left Scotland. Maria loves it too."

Maria appeared in the doorway. "Alex," she exclaimed, "thank you so much for suggesting us to Ms. Laurel. You don't realize what you've done for us. And to think we're living on the very farm where Cal's ancestor lived. It is so amazing. What a place for Tomasina to grow up!"

"I take it that you've each read your copy of Laurel's book. I hope it doesn't scare you off."

"Alex," Cal said, "my people, thanks to my ancestor Barney McCallum, have lived in a country where we take all this spooky stuff as fairly normal. And Maria? She's also retained the beliefs of her Mexican and Apache ancestors. I think we'll fit in just fine."

"I know you will," Alex replied. "But I just want to say that we really need to look out for Laurel and we need to protect Belle Rouge. I never used to believe in all this stuff, but after being on the farm and meeting Laurel, I think there's something to it."

"I can already feel it," Cal said. "I think I know how Barney felt... the way he felt about Claire Kilgore...I'm feeling that about Ms. Laurel."

"We must do things to neutralize all the bad that Genevieve started. I intend to help with that," Maria added. I have the sage, the incense...."

"Let's change the subject," Alex shuttered. "Have you seen the kitchen at Belle Rouge where you'll be cooking breakfast for the guests?"

Maria shook her head no.

"You soon will and you'll love it. Laurel wants us to come to the house tomorrow and she'll show you around and introduce you to Lenny, John Miller's deputy. He'll be staying here while John and Laurel are gone."

It had become a daily ritual for Laurel and John to spend the late afternoon together on the back porch, watching the sun set behind the hills. They were quiet on this particular evening, until Laurel giggled. "Wasn't it funny the other day when everybody talked about sitting in their old recliners," she said.

"And," John added. "How about all those old cars they all drive?"

"I believe our friends might be making some changes when they start working on our Belle Rouge projects. At least they won't be having much time to sit in their recliners." Laurel stood up, stretched and moved toward the door. "It's getting a bit cool. I'm going in. Are you coming?"

"Think I'll sit here a bit longer," John replied.

Sheriff Miller was torn. There was no way he was going to let Laurel go on her book tour without him. But he felt as if he were leaving their friends to the mercy of what was happening in Cedarville...the reappearance of the bird fetish, Nila at the hospital, Barney's descendant moving to the farm...and then there was Arianna Hull. What was she up to? Why had she made a couple of trips from Arkansas to Kentucky? Was she really looking for long lost ancestors and, if so, who were they? And why had she signed up to be the first guest when Belle Rouge opened as a B and B next weekend? Surely his chief deputy, Mike, would phone soon if he found out anything about her on his vacation at the lake in Arkansas. "Now that's another coincidence. Ms. Hull being from Hot Springs and Mike vacationing there."

Then there was this thing with Beth. Lenny reported that he had been in Louisville when he saw Beth at a restaurant. He happened to see where she lived. John felt badly about what he did next, but he felt he had to for Laurel's sake. He had a buddy on the police force in Louisville, and he asked him if he would mind driving by Beth's apartment whenever it was convenient. What his buddy reported had floored John. There were men coming and going from Beth's apartment. He had ridden with his buddy one night, and he caught a glimpse of one man go into the apartment. Now something nagged at Sheriff Miller. It was too dark to see the man's face. It was the way he moved that caught John's attention. Had he seen the man somewhere else?

John got up and moved toward the warmth of the house. There was no way he could tell Laurel what he suspected, nor what he knew Beth was doing. He made his way down the hall to their bedroom. "But there's certainly one great thing that's happening," he grinned. "Our baby."

It was after dark when Bobby phoned Alex. He was going to stay a few nights at his apartment just to gather up things to put in storage, he told her.

"Sure," Alex said as she hung up the phone. "And visit your girlfriend. You might as well not give up your apartment, Shine Bobby. Don't think you're going to waltz back in this house."

CHAPTER SEVENTEEN

MORE SECRETS

Cal was already at Alex's barn when she got there the next morning. "I'll help you with the feeding if I can get a ride with you to the track," he said. "Then Maria can have the car."

"I could use some help," she replied. "And of course you can ride with me."

Even in the dim light Cal could see the puffiness around Alex's eyes. Professor Ferguson's car wasn't in the driveway. "Something bad was going on," he thought to himself. And on the ride to the track it was evident Alex wasn't going to do any talking.

After Cal galloped Crimson Flame at the training center, he headed off to pick up a few more horses to take to the track for other trainers. By the time he got back to Alex's stable, he could see she was completely drained of energy. "Want me to drive home while you doze a little?" he asked.

"Much appreciated," was all she could manage.

When they pulled into Alex's driveway, Bobby Ferguson was already there. "You still going up to Belle Rouge for lunch?" Cal asked.

"No," Alex answered. "I have some unfinished business here. I'll call Laurel later."

She watched Cal as he walked down the road to the Ferguson cottage. As she was turning around she spotted Bobby. He was coming out of the woods and heading toward her house. "What did you learn in the woods today, Professor?" she said to herself. "Were you trying to figure out some way to tell me you're going to stay with your girlfriend?"

"Oh, come on, Alex," she scolded. "How could you ever let yourself believe a professor of psychology could ever be really interested in a broken down woman who mucks out stalls for a living?"

Her thoughts raged. "Every time I let myself get close to someone they leave...the trainer and even my parents. Then there's my birth parents. Why did they give me away?"

No one knew it, but Alex remembered bits and pieces of her life before being adopted. She heard her parents arguing. Was it about her? Had she been bad? Maybe they never wanted her in the first place. Was that why her mother gave her away? She remembered hearing the door slam as her father left. She heard her mother crying.

Then there was the shadow of a person in the corner of the room. Try as she would she couldn't remember if there was someone else in the house. Or was it simply her imaginary friend? She did have one.

"God there must be something terribly wrong with me. How stupid I must be for letting Bobby get close to me. How could I let myself become vulnerable again??"

Alex could feel her anger building to a boiling point. When Bobby came around the corner of the barn, she was waiting for him. "Who is she?" she demanded.

"Who is who?" Bobby replied.

Alex's eyes narrowed. "The woman you've been seeing. How dare you live with me and still keep seeing that other woman. If you like her so much, start packing."

Alex ran toward the house. "I knew you'd leave too," she yelled back at him as she slammed the door behind her.

When he recovered Bobby mulled over Alex's final words. "I knew you'd leave too."

"My god! What have I done?" Bobby rummaged in his pocket, found his cell phone and dialed Viola. When she answered, he said, "You've got to tell her the truth. She feels as if everyone has abandoned her."

Sheriff Miller had seen Bobby coming out of the woods too. He picked up his field glasses and watched as he walked toward Alex's house. "I'll be damned. I know that walk."

Viola was just coming out the back door of the Belle Rouge kitchen when she saw John hurriedly turn his police car around and head down the drive. He stopped when he spotted her. "Tell Laurel I'll be back. I need to go to Alex's."

"So do I," Viola said.

Bobby was sitting on the back stoop of Alex's house when the sheriff's car pulled in. His gut felt as if it had been hit with a baseball bat when he saw John's face and realized John must know what he'd done. And now Viola knew too.

Alex heard the commotion and opened the door. "What's happening?" she asked.

"We need to come in and have a talk," the sheriff responded.

After John and Viola left, Alex and Bobby sat in silence. Finally, he spoke. "I know what you must think of me. I've been so stupid. I'm not trying to blame Beth. I'm the one who should have known better, but I didn't say no when she asked me if I'd come to her apartment."

"Dear god, it sounds so sordid," he continued. "She said the first time was free. Please believe me, Alex. I haven't slept with her since we got together. Then I saw her at Eva Farnsworth's funeral. I never dreamed Laurel was her mother. Both Laurel and John have been so welcoming. And, Alex, I was so happy when she offered to give you some horses to train."

"I don't think I'll have to worry about that now," Alex sighed. "I'm sure that deal's over when John tells her who's been sleeping with her daughter. I doubt Laurel will ever speak to me again."

"What I did isn't your fault, Alex. It's all on me. I'm sure you'll get her horses if I'm not involved."

"That's just it, Bobby. I wanted you involved. I wanted you in my life. I saw us as partners."

"I'm so very, very sorry," Bobby whispered.

They heard the sheriff's tires peal out of the driveway, but they didn't know Viola had not gone with him until she came back into the room.

"Viola," Bobby said. "Alex feels as if everyone has abandoned her. Please, please tell her what you told me. She needs someone right now that she can trust."

"Good god, Bobby! You're talking about me as if I'm not in the room. I'm not one of your psycho examples."

"Viola, please," Bobby pleaded.

Resigned to the fact that she had held on to her secret far too long, Viola began. "Alex, please don't say anything until I've finished. I need to share a family story with you."

Viola took a deep breath and began. She spoke of her father's leaving her and her mother and her younger sister. She spoke of her mother's giving up the younger sister to be adopted by a couple she knew could take care of her better than she could.

She related the fact that she had secretively kept up with her sister. She paused a moment before she told of her mother's dying of cancer while in her late forties.

Viola saw the frown on Alex's face. "You'll see in a moment why I'm telling this story," she assured her.

"When I graduated with my music degree, I decided to take the position here in this county. Having all of you in my first senior class was such a joy to me. I watched you as you were working with your beloved horses."

"I'm sorry," Alex interrupted. "I don't quite know why you're telling me this."

Viola stared down at her hands that were folded in her lap.

"Please, go on," Bobby urged her.

"The younger sister that my mother gave up for adoption…it's you Alex. You and I are sisters."

Alex stared at Viola. "What are you saying to me? That you're my sister and that all these years have gone by and you never told me? Not even one hint."

"I so wanted to when I first came, but I didn't know how your adoptive parents would react. If they recognized me they didn't say anything, and I saw you were happy. I just couldn't do it."

"Even after my adoptive parents died you didn't say anything. I thought I had no one. I could have used a little support."

Tears began to flow from Viola's eyes. "I know, but I felt it was too late. I thought it was better not to say anything. Now I know it was wrong, and I'm so very sorry."

"I don't know how saying 'I'm sorry' can make up for a lie like that. It's as much of a lie not to say anything as it is to say something false."

"I have no excuses," Viola sobbed.

Alex glared at Bobby, "And how long have you known?"

"Since Viola fell and went to the emergency room. She told me then."

"I feel like such an ignorant fool," Alex screamed. "First Bobby lied and now to find that you've deceived me too! This is simply too much. At this moment I hate the both of you. Get out! Get out of my house!"

CHAPTER EIGHTEEN

COMPLICATED RELATIONSHIPS

After lunch John took Laurel into the parlor. "I have something to tell you," he said. "It's about Beth."

"Nothing you could tell me about Beth would surprise me."

"Oh, I think this will," he responded.

After he related that Beth had been prostituting, he told her that her daughter had been an assistant to a professor at the university and he was one of her clients.

When Laurel didn't respond, John continued. "That professor is Robert Ferguson."

"Did he seduce her?"

"According to Ferguson it was the other way around."

Laurel felt her stomach knot. How could she have been a better mother? How could she have handled Beth differently? She had no answers. She only had the facts John laid out before her.

"I don't think I'm surprised, John. I've never had any control over Beth, not even when she was young. She was always her father's daughter. Beth was sure she would be the primary person in her father's life after we divorced. Then he quickly re-married, and she felt she was cast aside.

"You couldn't help how she felt, Laurel."

"I thought we were finally going to get along when she moved to Louisville. Yes, we talked on the phone and for a while we had lunches together. Then once again she didn't want anything to do with me. I just don't understand her, John."

"She is a puzzle, but I think she gets herself into these messes and you just have to let her learn from her mistakes. Just know you aren't to blame."

"Oh, my god. What about Alex? Does she know about Bobby and Beth?"

John shook his head. "Yes, she does."

"How horrible she must feel. I need to tell her that this in no way affects our plan with the horses."

"I think she needs to hear that right away, Laurel. Viola just told me something else…a secret she'd been keeping from Alex. Viola is her older sister."

"All these years and she never told her? Alex must feel as if her whole world has caved in."

"She ordered both Viola and Ferguson out of the house."

"I'm going to talk with her right now," Laurel said.

It was over an hour later when Laurel returned to Belle Rouge. Laurel didn't know if what she had said to her had helped, but Alex did finally agree that she must talk with both Bobby and Viola. She just needed a few days before she did it. Laurel assured Alex that Professor Ferguson was probably telling the truth. Beth probably did approach him. Beth's father had disappointed her, so she looked to older men to find some sort of solace.

It was later in the day when Laurel, John, Viola and Jane gathered around the kitchen table. Laurel was the first to speak. "I must really seem like a heartless and uncaring mother, but Beth has always been vindictive and she's taken out most of her frustrations on me. When she started seeing Lucien Caulder, that was the last straw."

"Don't abandon her," Viola urged.

"I know how persuasive Lucien was," Jane added. "He said he would marry me if I slept with him. Then when I got pregnant, he left me. I couldn't finish college and my mother shipped me off to Savannah to have the child at my cousin's. Then Mother demanded I give my daughter away. I've lived with this guilt all my adult life."

The words poured from Jane. "Where is my daughter? Did she have a good life? Or, is she a replica of her father? Eva knew everything, and she tried to console me as best she could. Now she's gone."

Viola reached over and took Jane's hand. "We're here for you now."

"As are John and I," Laurel said. "If you like, we might be able to help you find your daughter, as soon as we get back from this book tour."

"I don't know," Jane responded. "Right now, you and John go on the tour, and Laurel please take care of yourself. This child you're carrying will be the only link the Miller family has with the future. We're going to find such joy with this baby."

John finally spoke. "We have one more day before we have to leave, Laurel. Do you think we need to go see Beth?"

"I think we have to confront her. But the minute she sees me she'll be on the defensive. She'll blame Professor Ferguson."

"When we tell her that Lenny saw her with multiple men, I don't think she'll do that."

"Should we take Lenny with us?" Laurel asked.

"No. He wants today and tomorrow off before he actually moves into the farm apartment. Said he needed to get a few loose ends tied up."

Alex knew she had more questions about herself than she had for Bobby. Hadn't she done something just as terrible as he had when she dated a married man? No, she didn't know he was married at the time, but Bobby didn't know that what he had done with Beth was going to hit so close to home. Did that justify what he did? She couldn't answer that. Was it better for Bobby that he just had a relationship with a prostitute rather than be in a bad marriage with someone? Hadn't she done something similar? She had shut everyone out of her life. What did that say about who Alex Jardine was? She had no answers and perhaps there were none. Maybe they had each done what they needed to do at the time. Maybe she and Bobby just needed to shut the door on the past and start over.

It was with some trepidation that Alex dialed Bobby. "There's a horse running today at Churchill that I might claim for Laurel, and I'd like to have your input."

Bobby was waiting for her when she got to the paddock. He managed a weak smile. "Which horse?" he asked.

"I want you to take a good look at the number three horse when she comes into the paddock. Just tell me what you see."

Each of the entrants walked the ring as Bobby studied the number three horse. "She's small," he said, glancing at the program. "This is her tenth start and she's never won a race. The good breeding is in the second generation." He turned to look at Alex. "Why would you want this one?"

"I think we can improve her. I don't believe she's been running at the right distance. She needs to go longer."

"This is a cheap horse. Don't you think Laurel would want one that's a little better," Bobby asked.

"She will be better when I get though with her."

Alex placed the claim form with the office, and they headed toward a TV where they could see the action of the race a little better. "I especially want to see the head on replay," Alex added. "You can see what happens a lot better that way. If we get her, Cal will pick up the filly for me after the race and take her back to the barn."

The filly broke slowly out of the gate and was several lengths behind the rest of the field by the time they reached the first quarter. She didn't begin to gain any ground until they started into the turn. When they reached the head of the stretch, she had two horses beat. She was gaining ground on the outside, but it was too late. Three horses reached the finish line ahead of her.

"I see what you mean," Bobby said excitedly. "She passed the winner after they crossed the finish line."

They got in Alex's truck and went back to the barn where Cal was walking the filly. "How do you like her, Cal?" Alex asked.

"You want the truth?" he asked. "Besides being small, she's got a crooked front leg."

"That's why she was bearing out coming out of the turn." Alex said. "But she's four years old, and I think her knees are set. I don't think that will be a big problem after we give her some TLC."

"At least that ten-thousand-dollar claim wasn't a lot of Laurel's money," Bobby said.

"Just wait," Alex replied. "She won't stay at ten for long."

At Alex's request Bobby rode with her to the farm while Cal followed with Bobby's car. It gave them some time to talk. Alex found it easier to talk when she had to concentrate on driving, rather than look Bobby in the eye.

"Okay," she started. "Maybe we've both done some things in the past we're not proud of, and I'm willing to put that all behind us because I think we can have a good partnership and..." she hesitated. "And maybe even a good relationship. But let's not rush it. You've got a few more weeks at the university before you retire. Let's give ourselves that time to sort of cool off."

"And," Bobby added. "Maybe we could spend Christmas together?"

Alex laughed. "Are you willing to go to your woods and cut down a Christmas tree?"

"But I won't be making homemade ornaments," he grinned.

"What about Viola?" he asked. "Have you spoken with her?"

"That's going to be a bit difficult. She kept living with a long-standing lie. I could have used her support many times over these forty years. I just don't understand why she didn't tell me she was my sister."

"I think she was scared," Bobby replied. "She didn't know if you'd somehow blame her for your mother's giving you up for adoption instead of her. She couldn't risk losing you again. If she kept your relationship a secret, she could still feel your connection. She was afraid you'd reject her and then she'd have no one."

"I think I vaguely remember her, but that fourth person in the family always seemed to be in the shadows. I didn't know who it was."

"Maybe your mind wouldn't let you see her because it would be too painful for you to come to grips with losing your closest family member."

"I never thought of it in that way, Bobby." Alex grew silent. But she was beginning to understand. How difficult it must have been for Viola, having her sister as a student and not having the courage to tell her who she really was. It would have disrupted both their worlds, especially that of Alex's adoptive parents. Perhaps it was best to leave the truth hidden. But why couldn't she have told her when her adoptive parents died? Alex had felt so alone at that time. Perhaps if she had known Viola was her sister, she might have never gone to that difficult life on the racetrack.

Then Alex realized something else. Her life would not have turned out any differently whether she knew about Viola or not. She would have gone to the track anyway, come hell or high water. She chose to do what she really wanted to do and nothing could have changed it.

But now she had a sister. She had family and maybe she had Bobby. But something still gnawed at her. She couldn't help but feel Viola hadn't told her everything. They rode in silence for a while. Then Alex grinned.

"What's going on in that mind of yours?" Bobby asked.

"I was just wondering if I might have some of the same 'powers' that Viola has. I think she'll reveal another secret when she's convinced I'm not mad at her."

CHAPTER NINETEEN

SUSPICIONS

It was late afternoon when Jane knocked on Viola's bedroom door. "How about joining me for dinner?" she asked.

"I'm not hungry," Viola replied.

"Oh, you don't want to pass on this microwave dinner," Jane smiled. "Please. I need some company."

Viola rose from her chair without any more hesitation.

The two women sat in the living room, neither enthusiastically enjoying her food. Then Jane pushed the mute button on the TV. "I feel like a fool," she said, "going on about my relationship with Lucian Caulder in front of Laurel and John. Why can't I let go of the anger I feel toward him?"

"Maybe talking about him will help you let go," Viola replied. "I just want you to know that you can talk with me anytime. And I know you miss Eva terribly. I can never replace her, but I can become your new friend and confidant. You know I'm really GOOD at keeping secrets."

"Yes," Jane snickered. "And you can keep them for a LONG time."

Laurel and John returned from seeing Beth, even more puzzled than ever. They sat on the back porch bundled together in a blanket. They knew this would be their last time to watch the sunset from their back porch till spring.

"Beth said she was babysitting with that little boy, John. I cannot imagine her doing that. I never felt she had any inclination to mothering another human being. Well…maybe she takes after me. I certainly haven't done such a good job with her."

"Will you please stop beating up on yourself? I don't know how you could have done anything differently," John tried to console her.

"Who did she say was the mother of the child?" she asked.

"Her roommate, the flight attendant. Beth said she wasn't expecting her roommate home till tomorrow. Evidently she has the child overnight."

"She continues to amaze me…in many ways. However, she didn't deny that she had been with Bobby Ferguson."

"But not for several months," John added. "Not since he's been seeing Alex. Now," he changed the subject, "you've got to get some rest. We leave for Nashville at noon tomorrow. You need to put all this stuff out of your mind and have a good time on the book tour."

Laurel reached for John's hand. "And you'll be with me all the way. But still I worry about seeing Nila at the hospital when Eva died."

"Maybe it was just someone who looked like her," John offered.

The jangling of the telephone awoke Viola the next morning. "Hello," she answered. "Yes, I'm leaving for Belle Rouge right now …. Bye."

Jane was making coffee when Viola entered the kitchen. "Alex called," she said. "She wants to talk with me this morning after breakfast."

Laurel had asked Maria to fix breakfast before she and John left for Nashville. She wanted one last meeting with everyone before they left on the book tour. Alex asked if they could delay until ten so she and Cal could finish at the barn and Bobby would be through with his eight o'clock class.

It was with some trepidation that Bobby opened the back door to the kitchen at Belle Rouge. Only John, Laurel and Maria were there. "I'm so sorry for what I did," he began.

"Stop right now," Laurel commanded. "No apologies are necessary. Let's just put the past away and go forward from this day."

Bobby wasn't sure John totally agreed with Laurel. His face remained stoic. "I really want that. I think Alex and I are back on the right track too."

Viola couldn't help but hear his last remark as she and Jane entered the room. "I hope that as well for Alex and me."

"I think you two will work things out," Bobby replied.

Alex and Cal were next to arrive. It was obvious that Alex avoided eye contact with Viola, but they were cordial, to everyone's relief.

"I wanted Lenny to be here, too, but he'll join us in an hour or so," Laurel said. "Could we get a report from everyone on how we're moving forward with our plans?"

"You now have a filly that I claimed at Churchill," Alex grinned. "I think I can improve her. Cal, Bobby and I have made plans to go to the November Keeneland sale to see if we can pick up a couple of other horses."

"Great," Laurel replied. "And I don't mind if we have a claiming horse. Those kind of horses can pick us up a check each time they run. Now, Viola and Jane...next weekend is the opening of Belle Rouge as a B and B. How are reservations going?"

"Fully booked," Jane said. "In fact I had to put some people off till the next weekend."

"I've finished the script for the tour of the farm," Viola added. "Laurel, could you spare a minute after breakfast to approve it?"

"I don't need to do that," Laurel assured her. "Just follow what's in the book. I know Maria's ready as you will see when you try her great breakfast. What about you, Cal? Are you ready to be the farm manager?"

"Gee," he grinned. "I've never had a title like that before."

"Anything you need to add, John?"

"No, Laurel. Except if you have any kind of problem, go to Lenny. He can handle most anything."

They were just finishing breakfast when Lenny appeared. Viola felt the hair rise on the back of her neck. She could see Alex felt something, too.

Viola and Alex remained in the kitchen to help Maria with the dishes. When they were finished Maria took off her apron. "I think you two need to talk," she said. "So I'll leave you to do just that...and," she added, "that's exactly what you will do. Do you hear me?"

"Yes, ma'am," Alex grinned.

"I don't know where to start," Viola said. "Except that you are my sister and I love you...I've always loved you even if I've totally made a mess of things by not telling you sooner."

"Yes, you should have told me, but I do understand why you thought it might not be a good thing for the Jardines. I've gone over and over it in my mind and I've wondered if I, too, would have had the courage to tell me. I just don't know. I have to say I'm very happy now to have a sister. However, I do think there is something else you haven't told me. Is it about our father?"

"Maybe I'm not the only intuitive in the family," Viola smiled. "And yes, there is something else. When our father left I found out he went back to eastern Kentucky. A year later he re-married. We have a half-brother."

"Good heavens!" Alex exclaimed. "Is there anything else I should know? Have you met him?"

"No. I'm not sure he knows we exist. I did learn that he's a lawyer."

Alex took a deep breath and slowly released it. "Well, you never know when you can use one of them."

"Now, I want to ask you something," Viola said. "What did you feel when Lenny came in the kitchen?"

"I noticed your face," Alex said. "I think we both thought the same thing. We'd better keep an eye on him."

"Keep an eye on who?" Maria asked as she came back in the room. "Is it that deputy, Lenny? I don't like him either. And I'm going to tell Cal to watch out for him as well. When they met the other day, I saw that Lenny had an instant dislike for Cal. And if anyone tries to hurt my Cal, my Spanish temper will put him in his place. You can bet on that."

"I've seen your Spanish temper let loose at those two guys in the track kitchen when they were treating a woman badly," Alex laughed. "I think Lenny will soon learn not to mess with you, or these two witchy sisters."

CHAPTER TWENTY

MYSTERIOUS GUEST

The driver Laurel's agent hired turned the black SUV into the rest stop near the Kentucky-Tennessee line. He followed Laurel into the building, but John stopped when his cell phone rang. "Hey, good to hear from you, Mike. Have you learned anything about this Arianna Hull?"

"I'll say I have," came the excited voice on the other end of the line. "Well, maybe not me, but my wife sure has. Before we left she noticed on line that a Mrs. Hull had a cottage for rent here on the lake at Hot Springs. She's gotten to know Mrs. Hull pretty well over the past week. And you won't believe this. This woman is the adoptive mother of Arianna. Seems like Arianna's husband and child were killed in a car wreck. She spent some time in a mental hospital after that and, when she came out, Mrs. Hull said she was determined to learn who her birth parents were."

It was the next thing his chief deputy said that rocked John back on his heels.

"John, are you there?" Mike asked.

"Yes, I'm here. Laurel and I will be in Savannah in a few days and I'll see what I can find out."

"What do you mean—'see what you can find out'?" Laurel asked.

"That was my chief deputy. When we get back there are some things he and I have to attend to," John answered.

Sheriff Miller had some reservations about leaving town just as Arianna Hull was coming to Belle Rouge. But he knew he couldn't leave Laurel and go back. But he would phone Lenny and tell him to keep an eye on her.

The first guests were to arrive at Belle Rouge around 3:00 p.m. Cal knew Jane, Viola and Maria could handle things in the house, but he wanted to remain close by. He would rather carry the luggage than have Lenny mingle with the guests. Anyway, the deputy didn't seem to be inclined to venture too far from his apartment at the barn. But Cal knew he was watching. He could see the curtain in the apartment move from time to time.

There were four bedrooms upstairs. The two couples would have the rooms on the west side of the house. Two older ladies were given the bedroom with the two twin beds, and the one single-bed room was assigned to Arianna Hull who was the last to arrive.

The guests had been given the choice of eating out for dinner or making reservations to eat at Belle Rouge. Only Arianna Hull requested the latter. With only one guest Jane and Viola decided they would serve dinner in the kitchen. They also asked Maria and Cal to join them.

The seating arrangement felt awkward. Jane and Viola were at the foot and head of the table, Maria and Cal were on one side, leaving Arianna alone on the opposite side.

Maria had prepared a light dinner of soup, salad and dessert. There was only polite conversation until they finished the dessert. Then Jane spoke. "Arianna, my cousin, Sheriff Miller, tells me this isn't your first visit to Cedarville."

Arianna stared down at the napkin in her lap. "No, I've been here doing some research."

"What kind of research?" Viola asked.

"I've been tracing family," was the only response Arianna offered.

"I've done a bit of that, if you'd like some help," Jane said.

Arianna glanced up for a moment to find both Viola and Jane staring at her. "I've found everything I need. Now if you'll excuse me, I think I'll go up to my room. I'm a little tired."

Arianna's footsteps echoed on the stairs, then they heard the door of her room close.

Maria began collecting the dishes from the table. "She's a strange woman."

"Yes, a bit," Viola agreed. "What do you think, Jane?"

It was a moment before Jane answered. "I think she looks a bit familiar."

After Cal and Maria left to go to their house, Jane and Viola lingered at the table. "What's puzzling you, Jane."

"Really, there's nothing. Well, it's Arianna's eyes. I know she hardly looks at anyone directly, but I did see them when she glanced up at us. They just remind me of someone."

Lenny had accomplished what he wanted in the two days before he moved in on the farm. He had gone to a restaurant in south Louisville, one where he ate often, that is, in the past few months.

He always got there early for lunch, seating himself at a table where he could see the door. Then he waited for her to come in. She had the child with her on this particular day. They sat by the window.

Lenny ate slowly, not staring at her long enough at a time for her to notice, he thought. Then the child dropped both his cup and his spoon. Lenny was on his feet in a flash and was quickly at her table. "Here," he bent down, "don't get up. I'll get his fork."

When he handed the fork to her, she smiled at him. "Thank you," she said. "You've been watching me," she stated.

"Sorry," Lenny blushed. "I noticed you eat here as much as I do."

"I guess neither of us likes to cook. I'm Beth," she offered her hand.

It was soft and warm and as she took his hand she seemed to caress his.

Lenny quickly responded. "May I sit down?" he asked.

"Sure," she replied.

Soon he followed her out the door and across the street to her apartment, but not before he maneuvered the child's cup into a plastic bag that was in his coat pocket.

That night as Lenny turned out the light at the apartment at Belle Rouge and climbed into bed, he thought of Beth. He had accomplished what he sat out to do. He would find a way to get the child's cup to the lab, possibly under Sheriff Miller's name. He had to know if his suspicions were correct. The results of the DNA test would determine his next move toward Beth. He hoped he was correct because it meant he would see her again. She had a most satisfying way about her.

CHAPTER TWENTY-ONE

PROMISES MADE

Alex carried the sale catalog with her as they moved from barn to barn at Keeneland's November sale. It was a mixed sale ranging from weanlings to broodmares and to horses of racing age. Bobby was in charge of the list of horses Alex made ahead of time, notating her comments as they looked at each one.

When they moved to the outdoor show ring, Alex spotted a small bay mare. She turned to the mare's page in the catalog and noticed she had placed a double check mark beside her name. Quickly she looked to the bottom of the page and saw that the mare was in foal to a stallion who was standing his first year at stud. "Look," she whispered to Bobby. "She's in foal to the stallion I believe is going to be a very good sire."

"If his stud fee is really high, we'll never get her," Bobby said. "Besides she's already produced a stakes-placed filly."

"Look at her age," Alex responded. "She's sixteen and not many people want a mare that age. And no, the stallion's stud fee is not high. His dam is a South American bred, and a lot of people here in the states don't particularly want that much stamina in a pedigree. I think he balances out all the speed in the mare's pedigree. Let's go in and try to get her."

Bobby could see Alex was nervous as they sat down in the plush seats. He knew she had never bid on a horse at Keeneland. She had summonsed up enough courage to go into the office and asked how she should go about registering to bid. They were more than willing to help her.

The auctioneer started the bid at five thousand. When no one responded he proceeded to lower the price, starting at one thousand. Alex didn't respond. Then the one thousand bid was accepted from across the room.

Bobby began to squirm in his seat. Finally, Alex raised her hand on fifteen hundred. Two thousand came from the first bidder. "That has to be the owner's people," Alex whispered. "They're trying to run her up on me."

Alex bid twenty-five hundred. Quickly the three thousand bid came. "Get up," she told Bobby.

Obediently he followed her out the door. "I thought you wanted the mare," he said.

"I do. Let's go to the back door and wait."

"For what?"

"You'll see," she smiled.

It wasn't long before a man approached them. "Do you want that mare?" he asked.

"Maybe," Alex responded. "What do you have to have for her?"

"Before I give you a price, ma'am, I will tell you her last two foals had crooked legs."

"You're an honest person," Alex said. "But if you'll shoot me a price, I'll see what I can do."

"How about two thousand? The stallion's stud fee was five, but we got it for free, being it's his first year and nobody knows what he's going to do. His breeding is not very popular and she's going to have a late foal."

"I noticed that," Alex said. "But I think I can manage that price."

After the deal was sealed they walked back toward the barns. It was evident something was puzzling Bobby. "That surely is a low price for what the others are selling."

"I know and maybe there is something wrong with her, but I think she's worth the price."

"What do you think Laurel will say when she sees how little you paid for the mare."

"She said to do what I wanted and that's exactly what I'm doing. Now, let's look for a couple of weanlings. I have money to go about fifty thousand apiece on them."

Cal sat at the large kitchen window that overlooked the expanse of the farm. He thought of the phone conversation he'd had with Laurel. He told her it wasn't the Scotsman who trained for Mrs. Lennox who was his ancestor. It was Barney and that he had taken MacCallum as his last name.

Cal could only imagine how Barney would feel if he knew his great-great grandson was back on the land where he had been a slave. Cal had heard the stories of Barney and how he went back to Scotland with MacCallum. He smiled as he remembered the story of how MacCallum had helped Claire defeat her father's horse.

It was true there was nothing left for Barney at Belle Rouge after Claire died. And it was very evident it had been a good move for Barney to leave. He and MacCallum became a team, MacCallum and MacCallum. Over the years they trained many good race horses in Europe.

Barney became famous and it didn't seem to matter to anyone that he married a white woman. He provided well for his family, but his children and grandchildren didn't fare as well. With most of their inheritance gone, poverty became the norm for Cal's parents. When Cal saved enough money as a jockey, he came to America.

But as he gained weight he couldn't get enough mounts on the Kentucky circuit. He garnered what he could as an exercise rider, living out of his old car when he wasn't offered a cot in someone's tack room at the track.

Then he met Maria at the track kitchen. She'd been living with friends, but soon they married, and with both their wages they could afford a small apartment. However, they were on the verge of being evicted when Alex came to them with the offer to move to Belle Rouge.

Cal would be ever grateful for the opportunity he was given. When he realized this was the very farm where Barney lived and worked, he knew he had been directed here by some twist of fate. He didn't exactly know why he had been led to Belle Rouge, but he knew he was supposed to be here.

He'd heard stories that were frightening about Genevieve, Barney's first wife—how her practice of witchcraft almost destroyed the Kilgore family. He remembered she had been killed when she fell into the fireplace and was burned alive.

Cal shuttered to think about it. But there was something else that occurred to him. He knew Genevieve had a son by Sumner Kilgore. Were there still people here in Cedarville who descended from that evil woman? "There had to be," he thought. Perhaps that was why he was led to return to Belle Rouge. Did Miz Laurel need his protection? He vowed to do what was needed, just as Barney had done for Claire many years ago.

CHAPTER TWENTY-TWO

ANSWERS AND QUESTIONS

The signings for Laurel's book went very well in Nashville and Atlanta and now they were arriving in Savannah. "Let's drive through the older part of town before we go to the hotel," Laurel requested.

"Sure thing," the driver answered, "but we're not going to a hotel. Your agent thought you might want to stay in one of the row houses."

"I'd love that," Laurel said.

They made their way to the waterfront, ate lunch at a pub, then headed toward the place where they were scheduled to stay for a couple of days.

"That's strange," Laurel said as she stared out of the window of the car. "I feel as if I've been here before, but I haven't."

"Stop the car!" she said abruptly. "That pink row house just across the park. That has to be where Nila and Jane's cousin lived."

"Drive closer," John told the driver. When they reached the front of the house, John read the numbers. "That's it," he said.

"How about that," the driver exclaimed. "That's where we're going to stay."

They would be in Savannah two days. During the first book signing John left Laurel in the care of their driver and made his way to the sheriff's office. He'd met him once before at a conference, and the officer was more than ready to help John in his search.

By the end of their stay in Savannah, John had the answer he needed. On his way back to the row house, he phoned his chief deputy. "Mike, what you and your wife learned in Arkansas was spot on. Now I have to figure out a way to tell Jane."

He was about to phone Lenny with the news, but before he finished dialing, he hesitated. His gut told him to wait.

The guests left after their weekend at Belle Rouge, all stating that they had plans to return. Arianna was the last to leave. Viola knew there was something she wanted to tell them, but she left without saying what was on her mind.

"There's something very familiar about her," Jane said as she watched Arianna's car make its way down the driveway.

"Arianna will be back," Viola assured her. "Maybe she'll feel more like talking then."

Bobby and Alex had the mare and the weanlings settled into the barn when Alex decided to phone Belle Rouge. "Viola, when are Laurel and John coming home?" …. "This evening? That's great, but I'll wait till tomorrow to tell Laurel about the horses I bought." …. "Okay, see you then."

Lenny returned to the apartment at Belle Rouge. He took a sheet of paper out of his coat pocket, sat down at the desk and began to study the document. "Just as I thought," he grinned.

CHAPTER TWENTY-THREE

LENNY

Lenny stretched out on the bed and searched his mind as to what to do with the information he had just received. But instead, his thoughts began to travel back to his childhood.

He was raised by a single mom who worked in the school cafeteria. By the time he reached middle school he noticed that, when she served him the portions they were either a little larger or there was something extra on his tray. He realized she did this because there would be very little for supper in their house, maybe just milk and bread. Sometimes she brought in the leftovers from the cafeteria. Once she was caught with the food and was almost fired.

He only saw his mother in the early morning and at night just before bed. The next door neighbor looked after him in the afternoons when his mother went to her second job, cleaning houses.

As he got older he wondered about his father, though he never asked any questions. He didn't even know who the man was. When he was in the eighth grade, he received his first clue as to his identity.

He was walking home from school when three high school roughnecks caught up to him. "Hey, little boy," he remembered their saying. "Who's your daddy?"

A man Lenny had seen about town was headed toward them. When he saw what the boys were doing, he grabbed the ring leader by his collar and threw him off Lenny while the others took to their heels. "See you later, daddy's boy," his assailant called back as he ran after his friends.

Lucien Caulder looked square into Lenny's eyes and said, "Son, you're gonna have to learn to take up for yourself." Without another word the man continued on down the street. He saw the man again a few nights later. He was in the alley behind their house in a heated argument with his mother. Finally, the man reached into his pocket and gave his mother some money. It was then Lenny began to suspect that Lucien Caulder was his father.

John Miller was a city cop assigned to the traffic detail at the school when Lenny entered his freshman year in high school. Once again Lenny was cornered by the bullies as he walked home from school. But when they saw John Miller heading for them, they scurried off. No kid dared to cross "Big John." From then on John Miller was Lenny's protector.

Lenny wasn't good at sports, but John convinced the coach to let him be a student assistant. He got to travel with team, affording him the chance to get out of Cedarville.

Lenny was also sure John got him a job at the ice cream parlor. The owner worked around Lenny's hours with the basketball team. For the first time he was able to help his mother with expenses, although she never gave up her second job until he was a senior.

It was then he began to notice a change in his mother. She was growing thin and pale. She was waiting for him at the door one day after school. She told him she had cancer and had only a few months to live. In the days that followed she instructed him. She felt she could keep working in the cafeteria for a while if he told no one about her condition. He should be able to graduate from high school before cancer got the best of her, but he would have to get a full time job. Their landlady, a friend and confidant of his mother, had agreed not to raise the rent. He was to go to John Miller and ask him to help him get a job in the Miller Construction Co. which John's family owned.

Lenny's mother held on for one month after his graduation. She seemed to be at peace when he told her John had gotten him the job. "Always remember what John has done for you."

When John Miller became sheriff he brought Lenny in as a deputy. But sometimes, Lenny had learned, you have to take care of yourself even if it means you may hurt your best friend.

In his spare time Lenny began to learn more about Lucien Caulder, the man he suspected of being his father. He learned the man had an obsession with Belle Rouge. And when Lenny began dating one of the girls in the county court clerk's office, she helped him research the history of the farm.

He had seen Laurel doing research on the farm too, but he had sworn his girlfriend to secrecy. She was not to let anyone know what he was doing. The girl seemed to like the idea they held a secret together. She imagined it kept him closer. And Lenny was sure his growing interest in Belle Rouge was safe with her.

What started as a mere curiosity about his father exploded into an obsession when John Miller shot and killed Lucien Caulder. It was as if all loyalty to his mentor melted away, but he knew he had to be careful. Something told him the sheriff possibly knew Caulder was his father. Miller would be watching him to see if there were any reaction to the death. But keeping quiet was no problem for Lenny for he had learned a long time ago that emotions had to be kept hidden inside. It was how he survived as a child and it would be how he did so as an adult.

For some reason Lenny felt an urge to check into the background of John Miller's family. His focus landed on John's cousin Jane. He had to be careful when he approached John on the subject. Then he hit on an idea. He asked John why he never went on to college. In the conversation John had revealed that Jane was the only person in the family who was interested in going. Casually he asked where Jane went and he found out she went to a college in Lexington and then finished up in Savannah while living with a cousin.

"Why Savannah?" he asked himself. The answer would not come until three years later. One day his girlfriend told him someone else had shown interest in Belle Rouge. Her name was Arianna Hull. Then he learned she had registered as a guest at Belle Rouge on the first weekend as a Bed and Breakfast.

When Lenny read Laurel's book he was sure he was on the right track. He had overheard the sheriff talking to Mike asking him to find out what he could about Arianna Hull when he was on vacation in Hot Springs. Now, with what this document that he had obtained confirmed, something was planted in his mind. He didn't know how or when, but he felt someday Belle Rouge could be in the hands of Lucien Caulder's children.

CHAPTER TWENTY-FOUR

FRIENDS UNITE

Viola and Jane finished decorating the house for the holidays by the time Laurel and John returned from the book tour.

"I've never seen such a happy house," Laurel exclaimed. "We need to have a party on Christmas Eve. No guests are scheduled for the B and B. Are they?"

"Not till the weekend after New Year's Day," Jane replied.

"How did Lenny work out?" John asked.

"Okay," Viola said. "He kept to himself most of the time."

Sheriff Miller didn't fancy himself to be anyone close to being as psychic as Viola, but he couldn't help but feel she hadn't told him everything concerning his deputy. He decided he would question her more when they had a chance to be alone.

Maria cooked a bountiful meal for the Christmas Eve dinner, and Jane and Viola laid out the place settings in the dining room. When all the guests were seated, Laurel took time to observe these people who had become such an integral part of her life. Before she could speak something flashed before her eyes. Both Viola and Alex noticed the split second change in her face.

"Is something wrong, Laurel?" Viola asked.

"No, no, it's nothing. But I suddenly thought of the Knights of the Round Table. Wonder why? Do you think it might be a premonition that we need to be strong in the days to come?"

"That we can be," Viola smiled as she caught Alex's eye.

"The table's not round," Robert Ferguson quipped.

"It is oval," Cal laughed. "That's close enough for me."

It was a bitterly cold afternoon when Laurel and John left on the second book tour. This time they would fly to Florida, minus the driver, as John had convinced Laurel's agent.

They would rent a car in Tampa, drive to Ocala, then proceed south to West Palm Beach, Fort Lauderdale and back to Tampa. It was to be a whirlwind tour that would last two weeks. Neither of them wanted to be away from Belle Rouge for an extended period of time.

CHAPTER TWENTY-FIVE

A NEAR TRAGEDY

It was close to midnight and Cal couldn't sleep. This was unusual for him. Normally he would be worrying about money during the winter months as the track remained closed during January and February and even part time jobs were hard to come by at that time. But now he wasn't worried about finances. The salary Laurel was paying him was more than adequate, plus she was also compensating Maria well for cooking at the B and B.

But on this particular night he couldn't shut off his mind. "So what was it?" he asked himself. What was bothering him?

As he tried to relax he thought of his ancestor, Barney. He was continually amazed at what this man had accomplished. He had gone from being a slave at Belle Rouge to being a renowned trainer in the British Isles.

Cal couldn't help but feel a little guilty that Barney's descendants couldn't build on, nor even hold onto, any of his fortune. But that seemed to be the way things were in life. Things traveled in circles.

He was convinced there was a purpose in his ending up at Belle Rouge. The circumstances that led him to this time in his life were amazing. Alex Jardine was the key. He felt he owed her a debt of gratitude that he possibly could never repay.

"You okay?" he heard Maria mumble.

"Fine, just can't fall asleep. I'm going to the kitchen to get something to drink. Go back to sleep," he kissed her on the cheek.

He passed the door to his daughter's room. From the glow of the night light he could see her peacefully sleeping. Cal didn't turn on the kitchen light. He didn't need to. Maria had night lights in every room. "Maybe another superstition of hers," he smiled.

He brewed some decaf and when it was ready he sat down at the kitchen table. From the double window he could see Alex's farm. It was almost like a picture postcard. The farmhouse and the barns silhouetted against the full moon sky and a blanket of snow just deep enough to cover the grass of the fields.

"Just think," he said to himself, "at one time the Belle Rouge property was made up of all three farms, Laurel's, Robert Ferguson's and Alex's. He realized Barney must have known all of it like the back of his hand. He must have loved it almost as much as he loved Claire. Barney promised her he would take care of it and her, but in the end, he couldn't.

"Was that it?" he asked himself. "Barney had failed in his promise. Was he, Cal now going to have to help protect Claire's descendant, Laurel, and Belle Rouge? "But how and why?" he again questioned.

Just then he saw something flicker next to the barn where Alex kept the young horses. The light grew brighter against the darkness of the barn wall. There was somebody there in the shadows.

Cal jumped to his feet. "Maria," he yelled. "Call the fire department! Then call Alex. Her barn's on fire."

He took time only to grab his windbreaker. He flung open the back door, jumped from the porch and ran toward the barn. Snow was packing into his slippers and his lungs were bursting in the freezing air.

He knew the horses were in the stalls on the far end from the blaze. Cal struggled with the frozen latch. The horses were screaming. Finally, with all his might he struck the latch and it gave way.

No time for a halter, he grabbed a rope and opened the stall door. Reluctant to leave the perceived safety of its stall the colt backed into a corner, stood on its hind legs and pawed the air.

"Damn it! I'm trying to save you," he yelled.

When the horse settled on all fours, Cal looped the rope around its neck and tugged the frightened animal toward the stall door. As they passed the adjacent stall, he unlatched it. "Come on boy," he urged the second horse. The horse bolted from his stall and remarkably followed them to the safety of the paddock where Cal locked them in.

He ran back to the end of the barn where the fire was beginning to creep along the covered walkway that led to the barn where most of the horses were kept. As he ran, he noticed footprints much larger than his. He would follow them later. Now he had to somehow knock down the roof of the walkway or else the fire would reach the other barn.

The jingling of the telephone awakened Alex. "What?" she cried. She looked out the bedroom window to see the flames enveloping the wall of the smaller barn. She saw Cal placing a ladder against the second barn. Alex knew immediately what he was trying to do. "Bobby, wake up! The barn's on fire!"

Cal was already on the roof when they got there. He was pounding on the walkway roof with a sledge hammer.

"What can we do?" she screamed.

"Knock down the posts that hold up the walkway roof."

Bobby placed his shoulder against the post and on his third try, it fell. Alex did the same with the second post.

They heard the sirens, then saw the fire truck turn into the drive and come to a halt. In seconds, the crew had the hoses out spraying down the flames.

When there were only smoldering ashes left of the walkway, the chief spoke to Alex, Robert and Cal. "We were lucky tonight. We had a late meeting at the firehouse, then we got into a poker game. Most of the crew was at the firehouse when the call came in. That's how we got here so fast."

Alex caught her breath. "We were lucky Cal got here so fast," she said.

"I couldn't sleep so I was sitting at the kitchen table and saw the fire ignite," Cal said.

"Do any of you have any idea how it started?" the chief asked.

"No," all three answered.

"We'll start an investigation tomorrow," the chief responded. "You all need to get back in where it's warm. Barn fires are usually started somewhere in the wiring. We'll figure it out tomorrow," he repeated.

"Thanks, Cal," was all Alex could manage.

As Cal made his way back toward the cottage, he once again spotted the other footprints. They led toward the woods at the back of the Ferguson farm. "I bet that's not where they end up," he said to himself.

The next morning deputy Mike phoned to set up a time to meet with Cal. Before the deputy arrived Cal took time to contact Alex to ask her about Mike. She reported he was a good guy and to call Viola and ask her about him because he had been one of her favorite students. That was enough for Cal. He decided he would confide his suspicions to Mike.

When the two men sat down at the kitchen table and Cal had offered Mike some of the coffee Maria had made before she went to Belle Rouge, Cal initiated the conversation.

"I saw a set of footprints at the barn last night, and early this morning I followed them to the woods behind the house. When they reached the woods there was an attempt to brush them away, but I'm pretty good at tracking. They led back toward Belle Rouge. When I saw that, I didn't track any farther."

Mike took a sip of his coffee, watching Cal's hesitation over the rim of his cup. "Do you think you might know whose footprints they are?"

"I have my suspicions," Cal answered, waiting for some sign from Mike.

Mike placed the coffee cup on the table and took a deep breath. "You believe they're Lenny's footprints."

Cal nodded. "But I don't see how someone who's a deputy sheriff would be stupid enough to set a barn on fire when there was snow on the ground."

Mike grinned. "It's Lenny we're talking about. He's not the brightest bulb."

"Then why did John Miller choose him to be one of his deputies?" Cal asked.

"John's always had a soft spot where Lenny's concerned. I think I'd say it's a blind spot. John started protecting him when Lenny was bullied in high school. I think he gave him this job because he felt sorry for him. When Lenny makes mistakes we all cover for him. But not this time. He's gone too far."

"But why Alex's barn? What does he have against her?"

"I don't think it was Alex. I think he was going after Laurel's horses."

"I don't understand," Cal responded.

Again Mike took a deep breath. "You know that part in Laurel's book where the sheriff shoots Lucien Caulder? That really did happen. When John had to do that to protect Laurel, something happened between Lenny and John, though I don't think John realized it. But I could see it in Lenny."

Now Mike leaned toward Cal and in a hushed voice he whispered. "I think Lucien Caulder was Lenny's father."

"Laurel used their real names in her book." Cal said. "That must have really set Lenny off."

"Caulder always thought Belle Rouge rightfully belonged to him because his ancestors were Sumner Kilgore and the slave woman Genevieve."

"How did you know Laurel's book was so close to the truth?" Cal asked again.

"This is just between you and me," Mike said. "My wife did some investigation into the birth certificates of the county. No father was listed on Lenny's birth certificate. But I think a lot of people believed it was Caulder."

"Are you going to tell John we believe Lenny set the fire?"

"I have to," Mike sighed. "And it might just cost me my friendship with John."

John left Laurel sleeping in their motel room. This had been the first night she'd slept well since they'd been on the book tour. When he got to the lobby, instead of stopping at the breakfast bar he turned the opposite direction and made his way to the pool.

He sat down in one of the lounge chairs, leaned back, letting the sun shine on his face. "Better make the most of this," he told himself. Soon it would be back to Kentucky and the cold.

He had almost dozed off when his cell phone buzzed. "Hey, Mike, how are things going?"

John listened, letting Mike finish the story before he responded. His tone was low, almost inaudible. "I'll take care of this as soon as we get back, day after tomorrow. Don't do anything till I get there. Do you hear me?" .... "Bye, Mike. And thanks."

When he got back to the hotel room Laurel was awake and talking on her phone. "Okay, Beth. I'll see you when we get back."

"Everything all right?" John asked.

"I guess so," Laurel responded. "Seems as if Beth is engaged to your deputy, Lenny."

CHAPTER TWENTY-SIX

THE CULPRIT

Alex and Bobby were surveying the damage at the barn. "Not as bad as it looked last night," Bobby said. "There's only damage on the front two stalls and the walkway. It won't be much trouble to rebuild."

"I was thinking of doing some remodeling anyway," Alex said. "What if we extended the walkway to the same width of the two barns and enclosed it. We'd have plenty of space for an arena to break the yearlings."

"I think that's a marvelous idea."

"I'm just so thankful Cal spotted the fire," Alex added. "We could have lost everything, horses included."

As they walked back to the warmth of the house, Alex knew Bobby was debating on saying something else. "What's on your mind?" she asked.

"I have the distinct feeling that Cal knows something he's not telling us."

"Cal helped me feed this morning," Alex answered, "but he seemed to be in a hurry. Then I saw Mike's car in his driveway just before noon. A little later I saw them walking toward the woods."

Bobby frowned. "I assume they'll fill us in a little later."

Viola, Jane and Maria were at Belle Rouge making plans for the weekend bookings at the B and B.

Jane looked over the list. "We have full occupancy in both February and March," she smiled. "The reservations are coming in from wherever Laurel has gone on her book tour and it's not even warm weather yet."

"Oh," Maria added with certainty, "we'll be booked full every month. "And I'm just so happy Alex's barn didn't catch on fire while we had guests."

"That fire was rather a strange occurrence. Don't you think?" Viola asked.

"Yes, and Cal and Deputy Mike went to the woods this morning, like they were tracking something."

"Or somebody," Viola replied. "Maria, did they double back here to Belle Rouge?"

"They didn't come into the house, but I did see the deputy's car come in the driveway. He went to the apartment where Lenny was 'supposed' to be, but he never answered the door and the deputy's car left."

"I thought Lenny was supposed to be watching things here at Belle Rouge," Jane said.

"I don't trust Lenny one bit," Viola frowned.

Jane and Maria nodded in agreement.

CHAPTER TWENTY-SEVEN

LIKE FATHER, LIKE SON?

The book tour in the South was finished and John was grateful it was over. Laurel never mentioned it if she were tired, but he could tell by her face that she was.

John was just turning off the interstate at the Cedarville exit when his phone rang. Mike's name came up on caller ID. Only after they reached Belle Rouge and he had helped Laurel into the house did he return Mike's call.

When he heard what Mike reported, John felt the breath sucked out of him. "Lenny's sitting on the railroad bridge over the river," Mike said. "When we approached him he threatened to jump. Says he'll only talk to you."

In minutes Sheriff Miller was carefully making his way toward his troubled deputy. "Lenny," he said as he sat down by him halfway across the bridge, "how can I help you?"

"It's too late," Lenny whispered.

"It's never too late," Miller answered. After a pause he continued. "You set the fire at Alex's barn. Didn't you Lenny? Can you tell me why?"

Lenny shrugged his shoulders.

"Did Alex do something to you?"

Lenny shook his head no.

"Bobby Ferguson?"

Again he shook his head.

"Those were Laurel's horses. It has to be her."

Tears welled up in Lenny's eyes.

"Did Laurel do something to you?"

"She's on my property."

"Belle Rouge is yours?"

Lenny turned to face John, the anger flaring on his face. "That land rightfully belonged to my father!"

"I don't understand who you're talking about, Lenny."

"Belle Rouge belonged to my father, Lucien Caulder, and now it should be mine."

"That's not right, Lenny."

"What's not right is that you shot my father!"

"No, no, no," John Miller cried. "I didn't shoot your father, Lenny. I am your father."

If someone were asked to describe Sheriff John Miller, several words would readily come to mind: responsible, dependable, good at his job. But on the other hand some would say: hard to read, quiet and somewhat aloof. These traits allowed him to keep his personal life a secret too.

He and Lenny's mother were in the same class in high school and it was at the graduation party when things got a little out of hand. Sure John had a few drinks on occasion after he turned eighteen, but he had never drunk as much as he did on that night.

Lenny's mom also had a few too many at the party. Maybe it was because John, the captain of the basketball team, was paying her a lot of attention and God knows not a lot of boys took notice of the shy girl from the poor side of town. But she let her guard down that night and Lenny was conceived in the back seat of John Miller's Chevy.

When she told John she was pregnant, he agreed to help her all he could financially, but he asked her to keep their secret and very well she did. She kept it even when people whispered that Lucien Caulder might be Lenny's father.

Maybe, she reasoned, if people thought Lucien Caulder was the father of her child, why not let him into her life. Over the years they had an on-again, off-again affair. It meant nothing to her and certainly, she surmised, it didn't mean anything to him. He was just company on a lonely night.

Lenny had seen him in their house. She knew he would reason that Caulder was his father. Though it grieved her to deceive her child, it did help her keep John Miller's secret. That was important to her. John Miller was a good man and she in no way wanted to tarnish his reputation.

And she knew she could bare whatever shame the residents of Cedarville placed upon her. Little did she realize what it would do to her son. Lucien Caulder's obsession with Belle Rouge had become Lenny's obsession too.

CHAPTER TWENTY-EIGHT

THE MILLERS

John Miller was now both sheriff and father. The law must be upheld, but the son must be helped. When Alex didn't press charges and with the consent of the judge, Lenny was placed in a psychiatric hospital instead of jail. Robert Ferguson recommended a doctor, and after some weeks of therapy, Lenny was to be released into John's custody.

"Do you want me to go with you?" Laurel had asked.

"No, this is something I have to do by myself," he said. He paused as he opened the door to leave Belle Rouge. "Have I told you how much I love you, Laurel? And how thankful I am you've forgiven me?"

"Oh, John, there's nothing to forgive on my part. Each of us has done something we wish we could do over. And," she added, "the most difficult thing is that you need to forgive yourself."

"I know," he whispered. "I'm picking Lenny up today from the hospital. Are you sure it's okay if he stays here in the apartment?"

"I'm sure," Laurel answered. "At least we can keep a close eye on him if he's here."

Arianna Hull was driving back to Kentucky, but this time she planned on an extended stay. She thought she might even buy some property in Cedarville.

After her husband and child were killed in the automobile accident, she had moved back in with her adoptive mother. She needed the closeness of her mother after such a horrific incident, but now she was feeling more secure and knew it was time to move forward and make some changes.

Oddly enough, Laurel's Mackenzie's book had given her the nudge to move on with her own life. In Laurel's bio on the book cover she wrote about wanting to change her life, which she did by moving to Cedarville. Arianna was beginning to believe she could do that too.

When her adoptive mother sold their family home and moved into a condo, Arianna knew the time had come. She packed her suitcases and placed what was left of her belongings in storage and began her journey to Kentucky.

She would stay at Belle Rouge for a while and then she could make up her mind as to her future plans.

Arianna was thankful Jane Miller had stayed a bit remote when the truth finally came out that she was her mother. Arianna had come to the conclusion she and Jane might share that trait.

She did realize she had a yearning to really get to know her birth mother, but that would take time and Jane seemed willing to let their relationship grow as it would. She was thankful Viola and the rest of Laurel's friends were at Belle Rouge. It didn't seem as awkward as it would be if she and Jane were left alone.

Jane and Viola sat at the kitchen in Belle Rouge, drinking their second cup of coffee. Maria had just taken a quiche from the oven when she grabbed the coffee pot and filled herself a cup, then sat down at the table too.

"Have you noticed something about Belle Rouge?" she asked them. "It seems to me that no one can keep a secret when they come in contact with this place."

Viola nodded in agreement. "Laurel certainly found out about the secrets the Kilgore family kept hidden."

"And you too, Viola," Jane added. "You finally told Alex she was your sister."

"And you, Jane," Viola said. "You speak more freely about your daughter." Viola paused for a second. "Then there's John. He finally told Lenny he was his father."

"How about you, Maria?" Jane asked.

Maria laughed. "I think my life is an open book. I don't seem to be able to keep my mouth shut. What I think is what I say."

John turned into the winding drive leading to the hospital where Lenny had been for six weeks. He was more frightened now to face his son than he would have been if he had to stare down a gun barrel a suspect was pointing at him. He wondered what would happen when he told Lenny he was taking him back to the apartment at Belle Rouge.

Lenny had to resent the fact that he had never told him he was his father. "Who wouldn't?" he asked himself.

It was true he had tried to take care of his son, watch out after him, but he'd forced Lenny to live without a father. And what had he done to Lenny's mother? He'd given her money regularly, but it certainly was not enough. She had kept their secret and now it was time to repay his debt to her.

It was early in the evening when Arianna turned into the driveway at Belle Rouge. She couldn't help but notice the buds were just beginning to appear on the maple trees that lined the drive. She rolled down the car windows and breathed deeply into the brisk air of the early spring. Somehow she felt she was home.

John Miller pulled in the drive just behind her, but he drove on to the apartment at the barn. John glanced over at the young man who sat beside him. It was a different Lenny he saw. The hardness that had once emanated from him was gone, replaced by a vulnerability. John vowed to help his son rebuild his life, this time on a stronger foundation—the truth of who he is.

After Maria served them supper she began the walk to the cottage she shared with Cal and their daughter. She breathed in the sweet smell of early spring. She thought of the people who were sitting around the table at Belle Rouge that night: Jane, Arianna, Lenny, John and a very pregnant Laurel.

"God bless the growing Miller family," she smiled.

CHAPTER TWENTY-NINE

BETH

Laurel had tried to contact Beth when Lenny was placed in the hospital. Not only were her phone calls going to voice mail, but when she went to her daughter's apartment there was no response when she knocked.

She was grateful when John volunteered to try to get in touch with Beth. Beth not only took his call but accepted his invite to lunch in the park across from her apartment. It was after they had eaten and had begun their walk through the park that John told her the truth about Lenny.

"In all those years you never told him you were his father?" she asked. "And all the time he thought he was Lucien Caulder's son?"

It was then John told her Lenny had gotten some DNA off a cup. He thought for a moment Beth was going to bolt. But before she could respond John revealed that he knew the child she claimed was her roommate's was really her son and that Lucien Caulder was his father.

Beth collapsed onto a park bench, letting her tears flow. She admitted to everything, even that she had been prostituting. "What will my mother say?" she sobbed.

"I think you underestimate your mother. Laurel will try to understand," he said as he handed her his handkerchief.

"What about Lenny?" she asked. "Was all the attention he paid to me just a ploy to get my son's DNA?"

"I don't believe so, but Lenny needs some help to get his life straightened out."

Beth couldn't look at John but hung her head instead. "I think I do too," she whispered.

CHAPTER THIRTY

THE PIECES FIT

It wasn't until March, the last month of the Turfway Park meet, that Alex felt Crimson Flame and the filly she claimed for Laurel in November were ready to race.

Flame was already five years old and had not made it back to the races since he was scratched at Keeneland as a two-year-old. Alex knew the task was daunting to get him back in racing condition, but she wanted to do this for Laurel.

Then too, Alex was a bit dismayed by the claim she made for the filly. The horse had a nasty attitude. She would bite and kick and she had a mind of her own when it came time to work. If she didn't want to do what her rider tried to get her to do, she would sulk and do nothing. Doubt was creeping in as Alex, Bobby and Cal drove north toward Turfway.

"Are you a little worried?" Bobby asked.

Alex nodded.

"I think we'll be okay. We may even finish in the money."

"That would be a miracle," Alex responded. "I hope the filly's jockey gets along with her."

"Won't be long till we find out," Bobby grinned.

Alex stared out the window. "I just don't want to let Laurel down."

"Even if things don't go well with these two horses, just look at the stock you've got in the barn. Thanks to Laurel and to Cal," Bobby said.

Alex glanced in the rear view mirror. "Cal, if you hadn't seen the fire I hate to think of what would have happened."

"I'm just happy I was awake." Though he didn't say anything to Alex and Bobby, Cal believed Barney had something to do with waking him up that night. He was even more convinced than ever that he had been led to Belle Rouge to protect Laurel, just as Barney had tried to protect Claire.

CHAPTER THIRTY-ONE

THE LOST IS FOUND

Arianna awakened early that morning but not before Jane and Viola arrived at Belle Rouge. She made her way to the kitchen where she knew Maria was preparing a sumptuous breakfast. For the first time in a long time, she was famished.

"Morning," Viola greeted her.

"Hope you slept well," Jane added.

"Wonderfully well," Arianna answered. "I'm ready for an in-depth conversation, Jane. I'm wondering if you might take a walk with me before we eat breakfast."

"I'd like that," Jane answered, "but let me get my jacket."

Arianna whispered. "I think you both realize I'm Jane's daughter. I believe this is the time to tell her. You've already guessed it, haven't you, Viola?"

"Yes, and I think Jane may have an inkling too."

Both Jane and Arianna were silent until they reached the path that led to the pasture behind the barn. "Then Arianna spoke. "Do you know why I keep returning to Cedarville?"

"I know you're searching for your ancestors, so I assume you've found them here."

Arianna nodded, but she couldn't speak because of the catch in her throat.

"Let me make it easier for you." Jane wiped away a tear that was trickling down her cheek. "Are you my daughter, Arianna?"

"Yes, and I know Lucien Caulder is my father."

From the smiles on their faces Viola and Maria knew Arianna had revealed her secret.

After the dishes were cleared from the breakfast table, Arianna asked Maria if she would sit down with them too.

Gladly Maria agreed. She was curious about this woman, just as she knew Jane must be. "How strange it must be for Jane," she thought, "meeting a daughter after so many years." She also wondered if Jane saw Lucien Caulder in her. She shivered at the thought.

"I would like to know about your childhood," Jane said. "I hope it was a good one."

Arianna began. "I had a good childhood. My adoptive parents did spoil me a bit, but they were strict. I knew my limits. The Hulls never kept it a secret that I was adopted. They also said I might want to find my birth parents one day. I really didn't want to for a long time. I was happy, especially after I met the man who was to be my husband. However, when our child was born things changed between us. My daughter had learning disabilities and my husband didn't know how to deal with it. As I devoted so much of my life to her, he and I grew farther apart."

Arianna paused for a moment to swallow the lump that had come up in her throat.

"It's okay, dear, just take your time." Viola consoled her. "May I ask your child's name?"

"It was Elizabeth," Arianna whispered. "Elizabeth Dwyer. After she and my husband were killed in the crash, I took back my maiden name of Hull. I guess I thought that might help erase some of the pain, but it didn't. I couldn't help but wonder why I hadn't gone with them that morning. I was usually the one who took her to school, but I wasn't feeling well that morning and my husband took her."

"You feel guilty about not driving her that morning, don't you?" Maria asked.

"I do," Arianna whispered. "I wanted to die with her."

"It was not meant to be," Maria said.

Viola nodded in agreement. "There's a reason you're still living. One reason is that you were meant to find Jane and your uncle John. But I think there is more you need to learn, and maybe we can help you."

"Jane," Arianna said, "I'm sorry, but it doesn't feel right to call you Mother."

"I understand perfectly," Jane replied. "Mrs. Hull is the one who mothered you, not me."

"Do you regret giving me up for adoption?" Arianna unexpectedly asked.

"I do, but I knew what would be best for you. I wrestled with that decision for years but I knew you would have a better life with the couple that was chosen for you. I was assured they were wonderful people."

"They were," Arianna agreed, "but I never felt like I fit in. I didn't look like them. I didn't have the same interests. I guess in the back of my mind I always wanted to know my birth parents."

"From what I hear you didn't miss anything by not knowing Lucien Caulder," Maria quipped. "Sorry, sometimes I speak too quickly and harshly."

"I don't mind at all," Arianna assured her. "But I would like to know about him."

Over the next few minutes they filled in the blanks for Arianna about her father. When they were finished Arianna took a deep breath. "Laurel's book held more truth than I ever imagined. There is something you said that did ring a bell with me. Jane, do you really have dreams as the book revealed?"

"I do."

"That's funny," Arianna said. "So do I."

It was close to dark when Alex, Bobby and Cal returned from the races. They were unloading the horses when Alex spoke. "I can't believe it. A second for the filly and a third for Flame."

Both Alex and Bobby stared at Cal because of what he said next. "Everything is falling into place."

CHAPTER THIRTY-TWO

A CONVERSATION

For the first time since late fall, John and Laurel nestled together on the back porch of Belle Rouge. John pulled the blanket around them and rested his cheek against Laurel's hair. "You smell good," he whispered. "But I'm not sure you feel well and I don't mean because you're so very, very pregnant."

"I'm a bit uncomfortable," she sighed.

"And," John added, "you've been really quiet these past couple of days. Care to share what's bothering you?"

"I'm fine."

John pulled back, placed his hands on both sides of her face and looked her directly in the eyes. "No, you're not. I think it's time you started sharing your feelings with me."

Laurel blinked, "I just find it easier to keep my feelings to myself. I know I shut down when I feel vulnerable. And I know I shouldn't do that with you. It's just what I've always done. It's the way I've survived."

"You've got me to protect you now. You are not alone."

Tears filled Laurel's eyes. "I did such a terrible job with Beth," she began. "Who's to say I won't do the same thing with our child."

"I say you won't," John assured. "You and Beth are so different in your thinking, but yet—and don't hit me for this—but you and Beth are very much alike in one way. You are both very stubborn. "

"Oh, surely not," Laurel giggled.

CHAPTER THIRTY-THREE

HEALING

Beth had agreed to spend time in a healing center in Tennessee and, sensing that Laurel wasn't up to it, Maria insisted Beth's son, Cade, stay with her and Cal while Beth was away. Maria also admitted she might have an ulterior motive in her offer. She wanted to know if this child had any of the traits of his father, Lucien Caulder.

Maria had been pleasantly surprised at the child's demeanor. He seemed to love her child, Tomisina, but he insisted that her name be Tomi and so the name stuck. She seemed to adore him too. And soon they were inseparable.

With the baby due in about six weeks, Laurel was spending more and more time in bed at everyone's instance. She didn't argue with them because her body was telling her it needed the rest.

No more book signings, no speaking engagements and no more helping with the running of the B and B. Laurel knew Belle Rouge was in good hands with Jane, Viola, Maria and Cal.

Her only concern was with Lenny's living in the apartment at the barn. She knew John would keep an eye on him, making sure he was taking his meds and, as John assured her, he seemed to be getting his thinking straight. The time at the psychiatric hospital was well spent.

And now Beth was in a rehab facility. "Are we all falling apart?" Laurel asked.

It was Viola who reassured her. "Sometimes we have to hit rock bottom in order to rebound. Both Lenny and Beth will be fine," she told her.

Laurel could only hope Viola was correct. "My god! What if they had gotten married before all this happened?" No, she couldn't let herself go there.

And what about Beth's child, Cade. Was this boy the next generation of Genevieve's line who would take up the quest of attaining Belle Rouge for themselves?

Then there was Arianna. She was Lucien's child, too. It was too much for Laurel to think about. She must do as Viola had suggested, not speculate on the future. The present is what is important. And the immediate present was this very active little boy she was carrying inside her.

Viola knew her task at the present was the healing that was necessary with Alex. In fact, Viola sympathized, Alex had two relationships to heal—with her and with Bobby Ferguson.

In her heart Viola knew the healing would take place, but it would take time. "Belle Rouge has turned into that healing place," she mused.

CHAPTER THIRTY-FOUR

COMING HOME

Alex, Bobby and Cal were still at the race track, but everyone else gathered for breakfast around the kitchen table at Belle Rouge. After they ate John escorted Laurel to the bedroom, but then returned to the kitchen where he picked up the morning paper. He was only half listening as Jane and Arianna were talking about the ancestors of the Miller family. He did notice that Viola motioned for Maria to sit down and join them.

Jane was responding to Arianna's question about one person on the chart. Preston Miller, she reminded everyone, was the high sheriff when the Kilgores first lived at Belle Rouge. But it was his wife's ancestors who were not on the family tree.

John began listening more intently when Jane mentioned she had no information at all about Rosland Wells, Preston's wife.

Jane explained. "I found her in the 1870 census, in the household of the people who had the farm next to the Miller's. She's listed as the housekeeper, but she doesn't appear anywhere earlier. Between 1860 and 1870 she must have come to the community."

"But from where?" Arianna asked.

"I don't know," Jane responded, but I did have a dream about her last night. Well, not exactly about her, but her name."

Both Viola and Maria pulled their chairs a little closer.

Jane continued. "I kept seeing her name on a wall. But it wasn't her entire name. The last syllable of Rosland kept falling away and the remaining letters kept being pushed together."

"I had a dream last night too," Arianna added, almost timidly.

"Go ahead, go ahead," Maria encouraged her. "You've inherited your mother's gift of dreaming."

"I saw a young woman on a train. She was so sad. Then the conductor on the train sneaked her off the railroad car. He pointed to a house not too far away and the young woman started walking toward it."

"Alright," Viola said. "Here's what we have. Somewhere between 1860 and 1870, a sad young woman gets off a train and the conductor tells her to go toward a house. Does that mean anything to anyone?"

"It does to me," John said. "I need to get a book from the library."

When he returned he instructed Jane to turn to page thirty-four.

She glanced at the book's title first. *"Untold Stories of the Civil War."*

Jane quickly read the few paragraphs, then related the story of something that happened in Roswell, Georgia. "During the Civil War the clothing factory at Roswell, Georgia, was flying both the English and French flags, claiming their neutrality, when a column of Union soldiers rode through Roswell as part of Sherman's march through Atlanta. When it was observed the factories were making clothing for the Confederacy, the factories were set on fire. Then orders were given that all the employees were to be rounded up and marched to the railroad where they were placed on a train and eventually dispersed in the north."

"That railroad," John added, "is the one that runs through Cedarville and ends in Louisville where the factory workers, who were mostly women, were taken off the cars and kept in various facilities."

"Oh, my goodness," Jane gasped. "I know from my research that the man who lived on the farm next to our Miller place was the first conductor on that train line. The railroad first opened in the 1850s. Could he have been helping one of the dispersed women from the Roswell factory? I know he and his wife offered a safe place especially for runaways from the orphanages in Louisville. Could he have also felt sorry for this young woman and directed her to his home?"

Unnoticed Viola had been scribbling on a piece of paper. "Jane, look," she said. "It's your dream. I couldn't help but notice that the woman Preston married had an unusual spelling of her first name. You dreamed that the last syllable of her first name kept falling. Look what happens when you erase that syllable and push the names together. She turned the paper around to show the other people at the table. "It spells *Roswell.*"

Maria gasped. "She changed her name so no one would know she came from the Georgia dispersal, but she left the hint in the name she chose, Rosland Wells."

"She was hoping one day that someone would unravel the puzzle and now, Jane, you and Ariana, and John have done it."

Ariana spoke up. "That settles it. I've been contemplating moving to Kentucky. Jane, John, I want to buy the Miller farm in Brookside. And I want to learn more about Rosland Wells."

No amount of dissuading could dampen Arianna's resolve. Both Jane and John explained that they had kept the farm in the family and they had renovated it after John's father moved his family to town and then they rented it, but for some reason no renters would stay in the house for any length of time.

Still Arianna was adamant. "Make me a price," she urged them.

"It will need a lot of updating," John explained.

"And one renter told me there was a ghost of an old woman in the house," Jane added.

"It's her," Maria said. "Rosland doesn't want anyone but a family member to live in the house, so she chased out the renters."

"Arianna, it could be expensive to renovate," Jane pleaded.

"I have money," Arianna smiled. "My husband was very smart when it came to finances. He made a good salary and he invested in stocks and bonds. Plus, he took out a one million dollar life insurance policy. I never had a job in the workplace, and he knew if something happened to him I would need money to continue to take care of our child. The interest on the stocks and bonds and his life insurance have left me very well off. I don't care what it costs. I want to live on the Miller farm."

"Alright, then," John sighed. "The man we sold Miller Construction to is a good friend. I think he could probably put his men to work on the house before they get busy for the summer. Should I contact him so he can get started?"

"Let's do it," Arianna grinned. "Just assure him that I want to be consulted on what needs to be done."

No one had noticed Laurel standing in the doorway. "Well, it looks like we might just have another ghost house in our near future," she said. "Should I get pen and paper and start a new book?"

CHAPTER THIRTY-FIVE

NEW BEGINNINGS

By mid-April many things had changed at Belle Rouge. Timothy John Miller was delivered by C-section, mother, son and father doing well. The filly Alex claimed had in turn been claimed from her and, after his old injury recurred, Laurel's gelding found a new job as a lead pony. And Beth was released from rehab.

Beth knew she couldn't go back to her apartment. She really didn't want to stay at Belle Rouge but she had nowhere else to go. At least she wouldn't run into Lenny for a while because he had gone on an extended vacation to visit one of his mother's distant relatives in New Mexico.

However, there was still a probability she would come in contact with Robert Ferguson. Not only would that be much too embarrassing for her but also for him and for Alex. She knew she had to make other arrangements, but she had no idea what they would be. The answer came from an unexpected source.

On the evening of Beth's first day back at Belle Rouge, she and Arianna went for a late afternoon walk. "Have you made any plans yet where you'd like to live?" Arianna asked her.

"No," Beth shook her head. "I just know I can't stay here very long, for all the obvious reasons."

"Renovations are almost finished at my house on the Miller farm. Do you think you and your son might consider staying with me?"

It took a few seconds for the offer to register. "Are you certain you want to do that?" Beth asked as they sat down on the rock wall that surrounded the Kilgore family graveyard.

"You and I have a lot in common," Arianna shared. "Did you know I was in a psychiatric hospital after my husband and child were killed. In fact, my adoptive mother put me there after I tried to commit suicide by swallowing an entire bottle of sleeping pills. I had such guilt because it was supposed to be me, not my husband, driving our child to school that morning."

"The survivor's guilt often happens," Beth tried to comfort her.

"I know. I learned that while in the hospital. May I ask," Arianna changed the focus to Beth, "what you learned while in rehab?"

Beth released a deep sigh. "I have abandonment issues. My mother left North Carolina to move to Kentucky and my father, in my mind, left me when he married very soon after their divorce. I think I transferred here to go to college so I could more easily punish my mother. I thought I could do that by having an affair with Lucien Caulder, but what I ended up doing was almost destroying myself."

"And now you need to rebuild your life, as I do, Beth. I moved here to reconnect with the mother who gave me away, and I really do know it was because she felt another family could give me a better life, which they did. But still, there's that feeling of abandonment."

"And then you feel like the whole thing was your fault," Beth added.

There were a few moments of silence before Arianna spoke. "Would you like to start our journey together. Would you and Cade consider staying with me on the Miller farm? And truthfully, I think I may need someone there because I'm sure the ghost of Rosland Wells Miller still resides in that house."

"You don't think she means to harm you, do you?" Beth asked.

"No, I don't. I think she wants a family member to live there. And that will be me."

"Do you believe there's a particular reason she wants you in the house, and what will she think if I'm there?"

"I think Rosland will like it," Arianna laughed. "Who better than two 'crazy' women to figure out what a ghost wants."

CHAPTER THIRTY-SIX

STARTING OVER

With no horses left to race it was time for Alex, Bobby and Cal to concentrate on their two-year-olds. They all knew their best was a filly. But she probably wouldn't race until summer during the Churchill meet.

If you wanted a horse to run early in their two-year-old season, the route to go was to break them in Florida, then move to Churchill, but Alex had decided against that. The filly was far too nervous to rush her. Alex's instincts told her that slow and easy would be the route to go. Crimson Feather, in her desire to run, would probably break herself down if they didn't take the slow road with her.

In May she finished fifth, then fourth at the Churchill meet. It was time for Ellis Park. No one could have foretold what was about to happen. Feather's odds were 5-2 when she entered the starting gate.

As Bobby and Alex made their way to the nearest TV so they could watch the race more carefully, they heard a horrible sound. A horse was flailing about, kicking the metal of the starting gate. They saw Feather's head as she reared above the sides of the gate, then flip over backward. The jockey jumped off just before she hit the ground where he would surely have been crushed beneath her weight.

The horse ambulance was pulling onto the track as Alex and Bobby raced for the truck. Cal was already in the stable area when they reached the barn, as was the track vet. Feather walked off the van but there was a deep cut running down her leg, reaching from just below her knee to her ankle.

"Can you save her?" Alex asked the vet.

"She didn't cut an artery or vein with the cut running vertically," he replied, "but she's going to be laid up for quite some time."

"Not if we can help it," Cal said under his breath.

When they called Laurel she said she'd seen it on TV. "Do the best you can for her," was all she could manage.

To Laurel it didn't seem as if she were destined to have any horses to run, much less a good one. John, as always, assured her things would work out. Yes, the filly would miss the summer meet, but maybe the easing off of the training might give her more time to mature, more time to settle down.

Arianna, Beth and Cade settled easily into the Miller home place. The house was what was called a half pen style. It was a two story with the front door at the right side. It opened into a spacious foyer. The stairs to the second story led up the right side of the entranceway then made a ninety-degree turn to the left. The catwalk that led to the remaining stairs passed under a stained glass window of blues and greens. One more ninety-degree turn to the left led to the two bedrooms on the second floor. Beth's spacious room was on the right and Cade's, the smaller of the two, was over the foyer.

Arianna's bedroom was a new addition on the main level with an ensuite bathroom. The house was not large but it was very comfortable for its three occupants.

Cade Mackenzie seemed spellbound with his surroundings. He was especially fascinated with the one remaining outbuilding. It had been built in the style of a small log cabin, but not with logs, with railroad ties.

After a close inspection Beth found there was nothing inside that was of a particular danger, and the building was close to the kitchen and easily seen from the window.

Cade spent hours inside poking around every corner and every box left inside. But one day Beth noticed as he came out the door he looked back and appeared to be speaking to someone. When she questioned him as to who it was, he said it was Ma.

"An imaginary playmate?" Beth wondered. "Or had the ghost made its first appearance?"

CHAPTER THIRTY-SEVEN

A GHOST APPEARS

Viola dug into her purse, desperately trying to find her ringing cell phone. Laurel and John had insisted she and Jane each get one of the infernal things, as Viola called them.

She found the phone in the zippered portion of her purse and answered it just before it went to voice mail.

"Hello," Viola said …. "Yes, tomorrow. I think we could. Belle Rouge only has one couple there this weekend and they only stay around for breakfast." …. "Yes, a late lunch would be good." …. "One thirty. We'll be there."

It was a few hours later when Jane and Viola sat down for supper. "Do you ever feel like you woke up one morning and the world passed you by with all this new technology?" Viola asked.

"Every day," Jane responded. "I missed someone's call earlier."

"That was Arianna. She said she had tried to reach you. She wants us to come to lunch tomorrow."

They arrived at the Miller farm a little after 1:00 p.m. the following day. "I have always loved this place," Jane sighed. "The winding drive, the house perched on the knoll, as if it's a sentinel watching the comings and goings of the community."

Arianna was at the kitchen door waving to them. She ushered them into the house. "Would you like to see what we've done with the house?"

Jane was totally enthralled with the renovations, but it was Cade that Viola was studying. He didn't go with his mother as she followed Arianna and Jane upstairs. Instead, he watched Viola for a moment, then took her hand.

"You meet Ma?" he asked.

Viola followed him to the small cabin. Cade told her to sit down on the stool by the door. He stood beside her and they waited, not saying a word. Then Cade's eyes brightened. "Hi, Ma," he said.

There were a few moments of silence. Then Viola asked, "Is Ma speaking to you, Cade?"

The boy nodded. "She says she likes you. You are quiet, like me."

"I'm sure I'll like her, too—especially if I could see her."

"No. Only me."

But a bit later as they turned to leave, Viola could swear she saw a movement in the back corner of the cabin.

The next Sunday afternoon Viola and Jane were once again at Arianna and Beth's home at the Miller farm. After lunch Viola and Cade, at Cade's insistence, went to the cabin to visit again with Ma. Beth excused herself from the table to do some paper work that was due the next morning at her job, and Jane and Arianna were left alone.

Jane studied her daughter as she cleared the dishes. She looked for something of herself in Arianna. It was evident she got her height from the Millers, but she had Lucien Caulder's coloring. The black hair and dark eyes were indeed Lucien's. Arianna had an almost exotic look to her.

Arianna smiled at her. "Why are you staring at me?"

"I'm just thinking how beautiful you are," Jane answered.

Arianna felt her face flush. "I've certainly never been told that before."

"Well, you are."

"I think you're also wondering just how much of my father is in me. Am I right?" Without waiting for a reply, Arianna continued. "Believe me, I've asked myself that question too, especially since I've learned more about him. I quizzed myself when I developed this obsession with wanting to live on the

Miller farm. But I don't think it's the same thing as Lucien's wanting Belle Rouge. I just felt I needed to revive this house. I think I want to honor Preston and Rosland. But," she paused for a moment, "I think we've revived Rosland's ghost too. I feel there's something she wants us to know. Mom, do you think she wants us to take her home to Roswell?"

Arianna saw the tears well up in Jane's eyes. "Have I said something to offend you? I hope you're not thinking I'm mad."

"No, no, it's not that," Jane replied. "You just called me Mom."

CHAPTER THIRTY-EIGHT

A NEW ALLIANCE

The next morning Arianna called Laurel and asked if she could meet with her. Laurel was startled at what her visitor asked.

"Oh, yes, yes," Laurel answered her question. "I didn't know how I could possibly find time to do any research for my next book or even what the subject might be."

"What if," Arianna offered, "we or you followed Belle Rouge with another novel about the history and ghosts of another house?"

"Do you have a house in mind?" Laurel asked.

"Your grandson, Cade, has the answer to that that question. I think his friend, Ma, is actually Rosland Wells, Preston Miller's wife."

"Arianna, you're a prayer answered. My agent has been bugging me to start writing again and I just didn't know where to start. If you're willing…."

"I would love it, Laurel. I need something to do with my time now that the renovation on the house is finished. I know Mom and I together can do that for you. I think we'll be making a trip to Roswell, Georgia, where we believe Rosland lived before she came here."

"Keep a record of your time and expenses," Laurel told her.

"I don't need any money. I just want to find out about this woman."

After Arianna left Laurel settled down on her bed, her son beside her. "I don't believe it's just about Rosland. It's a lot more than that," she whispered to the baby. "You've certainly been born into a strange family. Now haven't you?" she smiled.

CHAPTER THIRTY-NINE

ROSWELL, GEORGIA
JULY 1864

The three of them, a father and two daughters, left their family home for work in the woolen factory. The morning was already drenched in a stifling heat, but each of them knew there was something much more dangerous brewing this day. They knew the Union forces were only a few miles out of town.

"I don't understand, Father," said Millie, the elder daughter. "How can the factory owners expect us to stay here and work when they have moved their families to safety?

"We should be all right," her father assured her. "We're flying the French flag."

"A flag stands between us and those savages!" Millie sniffed.

"We do what we have to do," he answered.

Millie glanced back to see her sister lagging behind. "Father, what about Rose? How will she cope if the soldiers come to the factory? She hardly lives in this world as it is. She always seems to be somewhere else in her mind."

"Maybe that is what will be her salvation," their father whispered.

Rose was only fourteen and she had worked in the factory six months. Her job was gathering up the leftover pieces of cloth that fell to the floor as the clothing was made.

She listened to everything the people around her were saying. Most still believed the Yankees would pass them by and go on to Atlanta. But others said if they attacked Roswell the home guard was not strong enough to stop them. So, Rose did what she had learned to do. She kept her fear hidden and methodically kept to her task and waited for whatever was to come.

Rose was on the second floor of the factory when she saw the column of soldiers marching into town. Oddly she wasn't scared. She just wanted to find out their intentions.

She knew her sister and father were on the first floor where her father supervised the workers. If they knew what she was about to do they would have tried to stop her, but they would never see her when she slipped out the side door.

Rose was small for her age and she felt the officer in charge would hardly notice her. Four soldiers entered the factory and soon returned with her father.

She couldn't make out what the officer in charge asked her father but she heard her father's reply. "We are neutral, sir. We fly the French and English flag."

The officer dismounted and accompanied them back into the factory while Rose quietly and carefully made her way to another entrance and slipped back into the building. She saw her father arguing with the soldier in charge.

Angrily, the officer addressed her father. "Sir, if this place is indeed neutral then why this Confederacy stamp on the clothing?"

Her father had no response.

Quickly the officer ordered his men to clear the factory. Rose saw her sister move to her father's side. Something caught her eye. Two of the older women workers who tended a machine in the far corner motioned her to come to them. "We'll take care of you, Rose." Gladly she found refuge between the two as they were herded outside the building.

The following days would remain only a blur in Rose's memory. Flames coming from the top story of the factory, making their way to the second floor, then to the first.

Rose had no idea how long they stayed in Roswell. But one thing would remain in her mind forever. She saw an officer talking to another soldier he addressed as Doctor. "Here," he said. "Take this money and buy some supplies for your hospital. And please," he added, "try to hire some of these factory workers to help you with your work. God knows we need to do what we can for them."

Rose would never forget the Union soldier's kindness nor would she forget his face.

Then came their ride in a long line of wagons. The older ladies whispered they were headed to Marietta.

Millie and her father, unknown to Rose, had searched for her among the hundreds of people who were gathered in the makeshift camp, but to no avail.

"Father, do you think she may have sneaked away and gone back to the house to Mother and little brother?"

"I just don't know," he replied as he wrung his hands in anguish.

"She could decide to do most anything," Millie said. "She's been so strange this past year. I don't know what changed her—what made her pull away from the family."

"I know," her father said. "It's my fault. It's what I did to her."

"I don't understand."

"You remember that older boy she liked last year?"

Millie nodded.

"I was afraid she was getting too close to him. I confronted him. He left Roswell to join the Confederacy and was killed in the very first skirmish. Rose found out what I did. Something shut down inside her. She was never the same again."

Rose remembered being loaded onto the last freight car of the train. There was a passenger coach just behind them. The

conductor in the car caught her eye, and he gave her a smile of pity. They were headed north, she heard someone whisper.

Somewhere just inside the Kentucky border the train stopped. Once again Rose saw the conductor as he walked past the open door of her freight car. When the guards weren't looking he handed her a handwritten note. She slipped back to where the two ladies were sitting and opened the note.

"What does it say?" one of the ladies asked.

"My wife and I have a safe house. Try to get off when I do," Rose read.

Could she do it? Rose questioned herself. She had no idea where they were being taken. She had not seen her father nor her sister. What should she do—stay with the ladies or trust this stranger. Could she manage the courage to slip off the car? She had seen a man do it when they made one of their previous stops.

She asked the ladies for help. The plan was laid. The ladies would distract the guard on the opposite side of the car from where the conductor got off. Then Rose could have at least a chance to escape.

At every stop Rose watched for the conductor. The sun was setting when she saw him again as the train stopped. He began a slow walk straight west. As soon as Rose saw that the distraction was working, she slipped out of the open door.

The conductor did not look back, but in just a few seconds he felt an arm slip through his. "Hello," the kind man said as he looked down at Rose. "Don't look back," he whispered as they continued their walk toward the setting sun.

CHAPTER FORTY

THE RECONNECTING

Alex couldn't sleep. She got out of bed and went to the kitchen to make her morning coffee. The clock on the stove glared at her with it red eyes. 4:30 a.m. it read.

She couldn't make herself turn on the TV. She simply couldn't hear about any more problems in the world. Her own problems were enough.

With the hot coffee cup in hand she sank into her recliner. She decided it was time she met the thoughts head-on that were keeping her awake at night. First there was Bobby. The house was so empty without him. But how, she wondered, could she reconcile with the fact that he had slept with Laurel's daughter? Yes, she argued with herself, it was before she and Bobby got together. But she didn't know how she could ever be in the same room with them, knowing he had touched Beth just as he had touched her.

Alex did admit to herself that Bobby was horribly embarrassed when he saw Beth. But still, that didn't erase the fact that he had slept with someone young enough to be his daughter.

"Hell," Alex said out loud. "What did the girl's age matter?"

She took a deep breath. "It would matter to the university if they knew Professor Ferguson was sleeping with a former student."

"No," Alex corrected herself. "It would no longer matter to the university. Bobby had already retired."

She knew he was renting his old apartment on a month to month basis. Did she dare let him back into her home, her sanctuary? Could she ever let him back into her bed? That was the main question.

Alex took a sip of coffee. She was okay, she assured herself, that he came to the barn every morning to walk her horses.

"The horses." Again she spoke out loud.

What a failure she was in that department. To go from being ecstatic when Laurel hired her and gave her money to purchase the stock she wanted to the almost certainty that Crimson Flame would never race again.

Alex heard a faint voice in her head. "The filly will be okay."

"Maybe," Alex sighed. "The vet said it could have been a lot worse."

She put the lukewarm coffee down and closed her eyes. Then there was Viola. How could Viola have kept it a secret for thirty years that she was her sister?

Alex heard the voice in her head again. "Sometimes the only way to go is forward."

For the first time in a long time Alex realized she needed people in her life, especially her lover and her sister.

She dumped the rest of the cup of coffee in the sink. "But how do you do that?" she asked herself.

"Talk to them," the voice responded.

After a few moments she picked up the phone, dialed the number and waited for a response. When it came, she asked, "Maria, is it okay if I come by a little early to pick up Cal? I'd like to talk with you while Cal gets ready."

An hour later Alex and Cal were headed to the training center. Cal learned early in their friendship when to start a conversation with Alex and when not to start one. Today was the day he needed to close his eyes and catch a few extra winks of sleep and leave Alex to her thoughts.

Alex was driving on automatic this morning. Her mind was sifting through the talk she'd had with Maria. Maria had a way to cut to the chase, to find the bottom line when dealing with any problem. "A rare talent," Alex thought, "and even more rare was the ability to say what that solution was and do it in a kind and caring way."

"You need to act very soon to heal your relationship with both your sister and with Bobby." That was the bottom line in this conversation.

But what Maria said next was the very thing that made Alex push aside her reluctance to talk with them. Maria said she had noticed Viola was showing the first signs of dementia and she felt some other woman was about to come into Bobby's life.

Cal had informed Alex that Maria was picking him up when they were finished at the track. That left Alex the time alone so she could plan the next steps in fixing two relationships.

First, she phoned Viola and asked if she could take her to lunch the following day. Her sister readily accepted the invitation.

On the way home Alex made a stop at the mall where she made two purchases. Then she headed home to make plans as how to handle the situation with Bobby. She had said very little to him that morning at the track, but she knew he would be at his apartment in mid-afternoon because she had heard him tell Cal he was expecting a visitor at that time. In her gut Alex knew it was a woman.

By 1:30 p.m. Alex was back on the highway, headed to Bobby's apartment. Firmly, she knocked on his door. "The shock on his face when he saw her was certainly evident," she thought, "and so was his blush when he knew Alex saw the woman sitting on his couch."

Alex walked toward the woman and held out her hand. Almost timidly the woman took it. Immediately the woman winced then wrested her hand from Alex's grip.

"S-s-s-sit down," Bobby stammered.

Alex knew Bobby had been sitting in his recliner so she perched herself on the arm.

Bobby continued. "This is my neighbor who lives across the hall. She ah, ah, she brought over some homemade cookies."

"How nice of you," Alex said sarcastically. She took a bit of the cookie Bobby handed her. Then in turn she winced.

"Is something wrong?" the woman asked.

"No, no," Alex assured her. "Well, now that you asked, the nuts taste like they've been in the frig for a little while."

Bobby jumped up from his chair and headed for the door. "Thank you so much for the cookies. I really like them."

The woman immediately took Bobby's hint and, as she went out the door, the woman turned to glance back at Alex.

"Skinny bitch," Alex murmured.

The woman didn't hear what Alex said, but Alex knew she had read her lips. In a huff she crossed the hallway and slammed the door behind her.

Bobby paused for a moment before he turned to face Alex. "I heard what you said."

"It's true," Alex said.

"What in the world are you trying to do?" he asked her.

"Protecting my territory," she answered.

"That's what a tomcat does."

"Then I must be a she-cat," Alex laughed.

"I'd say you look like a pretty cute one in those tight white jeans and that red blouse. But don't you think it's a little low cut for daytime wear?"

"It got your attention. Didn't it?"

"I'd say so. But tell me exactly what the purpose is with this visit."

"Do you have to be hit in the head? Come on, let's go pack your clothes. You can decide later which of your furniture you mean to keep and which you want to give away."

"I take it that this is an invite to move in with you?"

"Bingo!"

She bent over and reached for his tattered suitcase in his bedroom closet. He moved to her and held her against him. Reaching around her he held her tightly against him. "I've missed you," he whispered.

She turned to face him. "I've missed you, too," she said as she led him to the bed.

An hour later they left Bobby's apartment, two suitcases in hand. "Your friend is watching out her window," Alex said.

Alex stopped on the porch, smoothed her hair, then waved at the woman. Bobby opened the truck door for her and took the keys she handed him. The woman was still watching. This time Alex thumbed her nose.

CHAPTER FORTY-ONE

GOING HOME

August was terribly hot and humid this year in Kentucky and not many visitors were registering at the B and B. Only two couples, both return visitors, had registered during the second week of the month.

Arianna came to see Laurel to tell her what her research had found for the new book. She told Laurel that August was the approximate time Rosland had left the train and gone to live at the Saunders' house.

Arianna had been mulling something over in her mind that she now shared with Laurel. "What if," she asked, "I go to Roswell, Georgia, see the places where Rosland was before she, her sister and her father were placed on the train for disbursement in Louisville." Maybe, she added, she could even find out if there were any relatives of Rosland left in Roswell.

Arianna had thought out her plan in detail. If it were alright with Laurel she would take Jane with her since there were few guests at the B and B. When Cade heard where they were going and that it might be the home of his friend, Ma, he put in to go with them. Since they couldn't talk him out of it, she wondered if they should also take Viola who could watch Cade while she and Jane did the research.

"I don't want to leave you shorthanded here at Belle Rouge, so Beth has agreed to come here to help, if it's okay with you."

"I think that's a wonderful idea," Laurel said. "Beth and I need to mend some fences and this might be our chance to begin."

"There's one more thing," Arianna said. "Cade insists on calling me Ari and I've taken the Miller name. Could you start calling me Ari, too. I really like the name and it's like making a new beginning."

"I understand," Laurel assured her.

CHAPTER FORTY-TWO

LENNY AND BETH

It was Thursday afternoon and Beth's phone started to ring just as she unlocked the door to Ari Miller's house. She fumbled in her purse and found the phone on the third ring. "Hello," she said without looking at the number.

"Beth?" came the reply.

She plopped down in a chair at the kitchen table. "Lenny," she sighed.

"Please don't hang up," he said.

After a few moments of silence, he continued. "This is probably the most difficult call I've ever had to make. Do you think there's any possibility we might have a face to face talk?"

"Maybe," was all Beth could manage.

"I'm flying home from New Mexico tomorrow and I'll be staying at Laurel and Sheriff Mil—uh, my father's apartment at Belle Rouge. Does that pose any kind of a problem for you?"

"No, I'll be working there this weekend while Jane and Viola are away. I-I-I," she stammered. "I think it might clear the air if we did talk, especially if we'll both be at Belle Rouge. We can't avoid seeing one another."

After the conversation with Lenny, Beth immediately phoned Laurel. "Mom," she said, "would it be okay if I came to Belle Rouge tonight instead of waiting till tomorrow. I have Friday off from work and I thought we might have some time to talk."

"Beth, do you know Lenny is coming back tomorrow afternoon?"

"Yes, he phoned and asked if we could talk and I said yes."

"Talk is good," Laurel replied.

"Thanks, Mom. See you in about an hour."

Lenny entered the airport in Albuquerque, but his mind was on Cedarville. Automatically he went through the routine of check in, security and finding the gate to his flight. They were loading just as he arrived. Mechanically he moved down the aisle and found a seat toward the back of the plane.

His mind clicked back to the present when he noticed a passenger two seats up on the opposite side of the aisle. She turned and smiled at him. She was an older woman, mulatto in color, pleasant smile and dressed professionally.

After the flight was in the air she passed him as she headed toward the back of the plane. "Obviously the bathroom," he surmised. When she came back she asked if she might sit beside him since no one was in his row and she would like to sit next to a window.

Lenny stood up to let her in.

"Thank you," she said. "Have you been in New Mexico long?"

"A couple of months," he replied.

"You've been troubled," she stated rather than asked. "I hope things are better for you now after you've been to Santa Fe."

"Much better, or they will be soon." he smiled.

"It's always better to clear the air, like the sky here in New Mexico."

Lenny didn't know why but he found it easy to talk to this stranger and maybe that was it. She was a stranger and he would probably never again see her.

He became aware she was speaking to him.

"Do you have family in New Mexico?"

"Yes, a cousin on my grandmother's side."

"Your newfound father's mother?"

"Yes," he answered. "In fact, I've just found out that the man I thought was my father isn't. My father is the man I was working for, the sheriff of our county."

"Strange," she said. "Sometimes who we think we are isn't who we are at all."

"Exactly. I realize that now that I've been in counseling. I was trying to be a man like the man who I thought was my father and he wasn't a good person. My real father is a very good person and I want to be like him.

"That sounds like a wonderful idea, Lenny."

"Funny," Lenny thought, "I don't remember telling her my name."

But he liked this stranger. Yet it didn't feel like she was a stranger. He felt from the first moment he saw her that he could tell her anything. And that was a very foreign idea for someone who had kept a lot of things to himself.

Lenny began to tell her his life's story: how lonely he felt as a child, no father in his household, only this man who appeared at times at his home, the man he assumed was his father. How he was bullied in school, how John Miller became his protector and mentor. How he betrayed the very man who had helped him. And how he had preyed on Beth to satisfy his rage.

But during his stay in Santa Fe and the counseling at the center, he had seen what was really going on in his mind. He had to go back to square one and retrieve who he really was and what he really wanted for himself.

He told her he had phoned Beth and asked if they could talk. He really wanted her forgiveness for what he had done to her. Now, he wasn't sure if he could face her. He might want to bolt and run when the plane touched down. He might want to disappear and never face anyone in Cedarville again.

When Lenny stopped talking he heard the woman and her lilting voice again. "She's Cajun," he realized.

"It's not possible," she said, "to run away from one's past. Though not running away is one of the most difficult things a human being has to do, when it's necessary to undo one's past deeds. Running away will not heal the wounds. They will only fester. Facing them is the only way to apply the balm of healing."

Her voice was lulling him into a comforting place, a place of needed rest. Lenny closed his eyes. It was sometime later when the voice of the flight attendant brought him back to the present. He looked where the woman had sat and she wasn't there.

After Beth placed her bag in the single room upstairs, she came down to sit with her mother in the parlor. John Miller was working late at his office and the baby was asleep across the hall, so the two of them were alone. Both women were keenly aware it had been a long time since this had happened.

Laurel knew the first words would have to be hers. "I'm really glad you're here, Beth. I've missed you."

Laurel's words seemed to open a flood gate for Beth. "Oh, Mom," she cried, "how did I let my life get so messed up? I know from counseling that I've been harboring such rage, but I thought I was a lot smarter than that. Then everything started to snowball and I couldn't stop what was happening."

"I know you were angry at me for divorcing your father," Laurel said. "But can you understand that I had to because he was going to move in with his girlfriend anyway. I didn't want you to see him do that. I knew how you idolized him. I didn't want you to lose your relationship with him."

"But that happened anyway. He pushed me out of his life and replaced me with a woman that was just a couple of years older than me. You had moved away and now I had lost my father too. I felt so alone, and when that happens, rage has room to grow and then the blame game begins."

"I know," Laurel choked back the tears. "I did that myself. I took none of the blame for your father's leaving us. But Beth, sometimes a relationship is not built on a firm foundation. We marry for the wrong reasons and the children suffer for it."

"Mom, did you ever think that we just might have chosen the right path so it could lead us to who we are now?"

"Sometimes you astound me with your wisdom, Beth. I hope you can see that you are a person wise beyond your years."

"I am certainly a person who didn't make wise choices at times."

"I think we can all say that."

In unison they spoke his name: "Lucien Caulder."

"What were we thinking?" Laurel asked.

"Mom, he was charming. His talent was seducing women. We were both vulnerable at that time. We were perfect prey for him and HIS anger. And for him, it all stemmed from the fact that he thought Belle Rouge should belong to him. He felt he was the rightful descendant of Sumner Kilgore."

Laurel took a deep breath. "I know you're right. But it makes me so angry that I was quick to jump in bed with him. Then I did the same thing with John Miller. It's a wonder I didn't lose him."

Beth laughed. "I'm not sure I'm comfortable with my mother telling me about her sex life."

"Well, it's a fact, and I might as well face my fallacies too."

"Again, I say, we were both very lonely at the time and you can say I was seeking revenge too. And it was against you, Mom. But now that I can see clearly, I know I wasn't justified in how I felt. We both were victims of circumstance. No, let me correct that. Let's no longer be victims. We're stronger than that."

"You're right, my wise daughter."

Beth took a deep breath. "But tell me how I face Dr. Ferguson. I can now admit that I seduced him. I was no better than Lucien Caulder."

"But you're alive, Beth, and you can mend any fence you want. Both Alex and Bobby will forgive, I'm sure of it. That is," Laurel added, "if Bobby can forgive himself and, in turn, Alex can truly forgive him."

"Dear god, Mom. We make any soap opera sound tame."

They both laughed and it was the laughter of healing, the antidote for anger.

"Now what do I do about Lenny? He wants to talk with me tomorrow."

Laurel reached out and took her daughter's hand. "Then you talk and you listen."

CHAPTER FORTY-THREE

TAKING STOCK

After they got back from the training center that Friday morning, Bobby, Alex, Cal and Maria sat around the kitchen table at Cal and Maria's home.

Maria had fixed an egg and bacon quiche with a garden salad made from the greens in her vegetable garden.

"Thanks so much," Alex said as she savored the delicious bite of quiche.

"Add my thanks too," Bobby added. "I don't think Alex nor I claim to be the best of chefs."

"Certainly not my talent," Alex quipped. "And I'm beginning to think that neither is training horses."

"Nonsense," Cal disagreed. "You certainly have a talent with horses."

"It's not translating to the winner's circle. I've got three two-year-olds. One is laid up because she went crazy in the starting gate, one has a breathing problem and will probably never race and one is simply too lazy to work enough to get fit to race."

"It's darkest before the dawn," Maria said as she refreshed their coffee cups.

"Well, I think it's time someone turned on the light. I don't know what else to do. I feel I've let Laurel down."

Maria jumped in again. "Ms. Laurel doesn't feel that way at all, I assure you of that. She understands that horse racing is a gamble and not just at the betting windows. Your fortune is about to change. I can feel it."

"Okay, then," Alex said. "Will you help in figuring out just where we are with these horses? I don't seem to be able to focus like I should. Maybe if we discuss each of the horses, we can figure out what we need to do to have a successful stable."

Cal spoke up. "Let's take the one that has the breathing problem. We really haven't had the vet check her out."

"Vets are so expensive," Alex said. "I just hate for Laurel to get a huge bill."

"But the horse is not doing you any good the way it is," Maria chimed in. "Spending the money for a thorough checkup could prove to be profitable in the long run."

"You're right," Alex signed. "It would really be stupid not to. Now there's the colt that won't put any effort into his gallops. I can't get him fit enough to run."

"I think he's hurting somewhere," Cal said. "Maria, do you still have the phone number of your friend who does chiropractic work on horses? Maybe she could find out if something is giving him discomfort."

Within two days they had their answers. The horse with the breathing problem had a guttural pouch infection that could be healed with antibiotics and the chiropractor found a problem with the sternum and a couple of the vertebrae with the lazy horse. She thought one more treatment could alleviate his problem.

Alex had discussed the horses' problems with Laurel, and she had agreed that it would be money well spent. Alex could finally breathe a sigh of relief.

As for Crimson Flame, she was healing far faster than had been expected.

CHAPTER FORTY-FOUR

A TRIP TO THE PAST

Ari, Jane, Viola and Cade had arrived at Roswell, Georgia, at mid-afternoon on Thursday. Viola and Cade sat in the back seat and periodically played his games and dozed. But just as they reached the outskirts of town, Cade became wide awake and began to look anxiously at their surroundings.

When he settled back into his seat he spoke. "Ma says not the same. Not home anymore. She ready to go back to our house."

"Cade," Viola cajoled him, "don't you want to see where Ma came from? I know I do and Ari and Jane do. Don't you think Ma could just ride along with us. Maybe she can even show us where she worked and where she lived when she was here."

Cade was silent for a moment, as if he were listening for someone's answer. "Ma says that's okay. Turn down the next street. We go where she worked."

"Will do, Ma," Ari said.

They drove through the center of town and then Cade continued his direction. "Over there," he said. "That big place."

"That's it," Jane said as she read the sign. "It's been rebuilt, but that's the factory described in the book John has."

Just up the hill was a small building that was the historical museum of Roswell. They talked with the volunteer behind the desk and Ari bought several books.

Then she asked the volunteer a question. "Are there any people here in Roswell who have ancestors that made it back after the people at the factory were dispersed?"

The volunteer picked up one of the books and turned to a page that contained a list of names. "I don't see anyone with the name of Wells."

The volunteer's finger scanned the list and came to rest on a name. "Do you think the name you're looking for could be 'Williams' instead of Wells?" he asked.

"We do feel she may have changed her name, not wanting people to know her real identity," Ari answered. "We know her as Rosland Wells. We think she may have chosen a name for herself that's a play on the name of her home town, Roswell."

"If you think she just might have been Rose Williams, there is someone here in town that I think you could talk with and I know she would love to talk with you."

The volunteer scribbled down a name and address and handed it to Ari. "I'll call her and let her know you'll be dropping by."

It was Cade's nap time, so Viola volunteered to stay with him at the motel while Jane and Ari went to see the descendant of the Williams family.

The housekeeper opened the door in response to Ari's knock. "Is this the home of Maude Williams?" she asked.

"Yes, Miss Maude is expecting you," the housekeeper replied. "She's in the parlor."

The woman led them through the foyer and into a room where it was evident the décor had not changed for many decades. A grey-haired lady sat in an arm chair, her face lighting up when she saw Ari and Jane.

"The volunteer at the museum said you might have some information on a member of my family," she said as she extended her hand to them. "Please sit down. I can hardly wait to hear what you have to tell me. I hope it helps to solve a mystery that has been in our family since the Civil War."

Jane took a note pad from her purse and placed it on the table beside Miss Maude. "Here is an ancestral chart of my family. Right here," she pointed, "is a Rosland Wells who married Preston Miller who was the sheriff in our county. We've come to believe Ma Miller might have come into our county as a result of the displacement of the workers at the mill here in Roswell during the war."

"That would be a miracle," Miss Maude explained. "Do you think she just might be Rose Williams?"

"Yes, we do," Ari chimed in.

"Let me show you this," Miss Maude said, laying out the hand-drawn chart of her lineage. "When my great-grandfather and his two daughters, Millie and Rose, were dispersed, they left behind my great-grandmother and her youngest child, Robert, who was my grandfather. As you can see, I'm the last of Robert's line."

Jane studied the chart. "We learned at the museum that your great-grandfather and Millie got back to Roswell. Did you ever find out anything about Rose? Did they know how she got separated from them on the train?"

"As the story goes, from what they told, they were not together in the factory when the soldiers came. They got a glimpse of Rose in the company of some of the older women who worked on another floor of the factory. When they got on the train bound for Louisville, they briefly saw her again at the last stop before their final destination, which was Louisville. The conductor on the train was speaking to Rose."

"It's her, it's her," Ari cried. "It all fits."

Ari and Jane quickly filled Miss Maude in on Rose's life. When they finished, Miss Maude sat back in her chair, a broad smile across her face.

"I was told that Rose was always an independent girl, always in her own world, with her own thoughts. I feel she was quite resourceful."

"And brave," Jane added. "To think she had nerve enough to trust that Mr. Saunders and his wife who did indeed help displaced people. I'm not sure I would have had her courage."

"What happened to Millie?" Ari interjected.

"Millie Williams married and moved away from Roswell," Miss Maude answered. "I have her ancestral chart too. Would you like to see it? I have it right here." She handed it to Ari.

Quickly Ari's eyes moved down through the names on the chart, coming to rest on the bottom line. "Oh, my god," she exclaimed. "This can't possibly be. It can't be."

CHAPTER FORTY-FIVE

THE TIE THAT BINDS

Ari tossed and turned, trying to sleep but unable to turn off her thoughts. The question kept playing and playing in her mind. "Should I call my adoptive mother and tell her what I learned in Roswell?"

Jane, her birth mother, seemed pleased when she saw the ancestral tree of the Williams family. It was almost as if some of the guilt she had of giving Ari up for adoption had been lifted from her.

But Ari was not sure how her adoptive mother would react when she told her she knew they had kept one important fact from her. Yes, they had told Ari she was adopted, but they didn't tell her everything. They had left out one very important thing.

At 9:00 a.m. the next morning Ari picked up the phone. Hesitantly she dialed the area code for Arkansas. She paused for a second then hurriedly dialed the rest of the numbers.

"Hello," came the response.

Ari blurted out, "Mother, I know who I am."

Bobby and Alex sat in their stable office, relaxing after the morning routine. Bobby stretched his arms and yawned. When he settled back down he asked, "What's your assessment of how the two-year-olds are doing?"

"I think we can have Feather ready for Churchill in September. October at Keeneland for Snorter. Maybe November for Mr. Lazy."

"You really ought to stop calling them Snorter and Lazy," Bobby laughed.

"I know," Alex grinned, "but you have to admit it suits them. You think up new names for them."

"How about Flash for Mr. Lazy? Let me think on the other," Bobby said.

Alex got up from her chair and reached out for Bobby's hand. "Come on. Let's go home. We had a bit of a late night last night," she winked. "I think it's nap time."

Laurel was in bed, dozing, when the jangling of the phone awoke her. "Hello ....You say you might have something for a new book? .... Sure three o'clock would be fine. See you then."

"Who was that?" John asked.

"Ari. She says she has something very important for the new book."

"Are you ready to start writing again?"

"I think so. No, I know so," Laurel grinned. "Maria has been so wonderful at helping with the baby I have very little to do...most of the time."

John bent to kiss her on her forehead. "Then I'm all for it."

"Aren't you a bit late going to your office?" Laurel asked.

"I'm taking the day off. I'm going to spend it with Lenny."

"That's a grand idea. Do you know how much I love you, John Miller?"

"Half as much as I love you."

Viola and Jane didn't go to Belle Rouge this day. Maria knew they were both tired from the Roswell trip and, since no guests were booked this early in the week, she suggested they stay home and rest. They were finishing a late breakfast when a knock came at the door.

Jane peeped through the window. "It's Ari," she announced. "Come in. It's so good to see you."

Ari got right to the point. "Could we have a talk?" she asked.

The three of them moved to the living room and Ari began. "I made the call to Arkansas this morning. My adoptive mother denied knowing anything about my father's ancestors. I told her I could fill her in."

"I told her about Rose's coming to Kentucky during the dispersal of factory workers and that she was your ancestor, Mom. I explained that Rose's sister, Millie, married and moved to Savannah, the city where I was adopted, and that Millie Williams Hull was my adoptive father's ancestor."

"How did she react?" Viola asked.

"She seemed generally surprised. She said she'd look at my adoptive father's papers to see if he knew."

"He had to have known," Jane said. "He and Millie had the same name—Hull. Dr. Nila must have known, too. I think she purposely placed you with a relative."

Ari got up and headed toward the door. "I need to go. I promised Laurel I'd drop by this afternoon." She turned to face them once more. "You know what all this means. I'm related to the Williams family two times through both Rose and Millie."

"Are you concerned about that?" Jane asked.

Ari came back and once again plopped down in the chair. "No, not really, but there's something else I might as well tell you. I haven't been quite truthful with you, at least not all of the truth."

"Who of us has been?" Viola asked. "Sorry, please go on."

"I've told you my husband and child were killed in a car accident and that I had to have some help with handling the loss. It wasn't just the guilt of my not being in the car that led me to go to the hospital. I'll have to say I had such a good therapist and she helped me get to the bottom of what was really causing all my grief."

Ari paused for a moment. Then spoke, "Mom, do you think we could have something to drink?"

"I'll fix some tea," Jane responded.

Ari looked directly at Viola. "You know what I'm about to say. Don't you?"

"I've known for some time, but I've not said anything to anyone. You can do this. It's time."

"Thank you."

When Jane returned she placed the glasses of iced tea in front of each of them. She looked from first one then the other. "What's going on?" she asked.

Ari took a deep breath, then began. "My guilt after losing my husband and child goes a lot deeper than what I've already told you. I married my husband to cover up something. Over the years I'd grown so resentful toward him and he resented me because we were never intimate after our daughter was born. I simply couldn't stand for him to touch me. Our lives were miserable. I felt guilt for not being in the car with them, but I felt even more guilt for being so dishonest in our relationship. You see…you see, I'm gay."

Jane paused only for a moment. Then she took Ari in her arms. "You're my daughter. That's all that matters."

CHAPTER FORTY-SIX

PATIENCE PAYS OFF

Churchill Downs' September meet opened with night racing. Every race was for two- year-olds. Alex felt Crimson Feather was ready to race and, with the breathing problem fixed on Crimson Delight, he was probably going to need a race before he was ready to win. But she thought she would go ahead and enter him anyway. There might be a chance he could hit the board. Then there was Crimson Demon, the lazy boy. Who could tell if he were ready or not. He simply refused to put anything into his workouts in the mornings.

"Oh, what the hell," Alex said as she picked up the phone to enter all three horses.

When the racing secretary's office answered, she began. "I want to enter Crimson Delight in race one, the $25,000 Maiden Claiming, six furlongs; Crimson Feather in race five, the Maiden Special Weight; and Crimson Demon in race nine, the $25,000 Maiden Claiming, one mile on the turf."

When race day came Alex didn't know whether to be delighted or horrified that Laurel had invited all the friends to witness the races. To say she had a knot in her stomach was an understatement.

Bobby tried to settle Alex down, but to no avail. Cal assured her they all had done the best they knew how with the horses, so let go of what might happen and simply enjoy the day.

The call soon came for the horses in the first race. Bobby and Cal each held a lead shank on either side of Crimson Delight. Alex felt Cal could handle the horse by himself, but she wanted to be safe because one never knew what a two-year-old would do when it saw the crowd that lined the fence.

Alex felt a chill of excitement when they entered the paddock. She'd been there many times over the years, but this day was special. She had a very important client in Laurel and these three horses were probably the best she ever had, especially Crimson Feather.

"Let go of the outcome," she reminded herself. Soon her mind was occupied with saddling Crimson Delight. Alex wasn't sure about her choice of jockeys, but Cal pushed to have Jimmy Collins, a veteran jockey, in the saddle.

"He really is smart and careful," Cal assured her. "And that's the kind of jockey you need with these babies."

Alex gave Jimmy a leg up. "Play it as the race unfolds, Jimmy," she said. The horses circled the paddock, then headed out toward the track.

"Well, what do you think, Bobby?" she asked.

"Guess we'll soon see," he grinned.

The horses approached the starting gate. Crimson Delight drew post number three. It was a full field of twelve which meant Delight would have to stand in the gate for some time while the rest of the horses were loaded.

The gate crew was having trouble with the eleven horse, but Alex stared at Delight through her field glasses. He was standing still, maybe too still, she thought.

The eleven finally went in and as soon as the twelve did likewise, the starter rang the bell. Just as Alex feared, Delight was not ready and he broke a full three lengths behind the rest of the horses.

"Well, that's it," Alex sighed. "The race is only six furlongs and he has no chance of making up the ground."

Midway down the back stretch Delight had passed one horse. Jimmy Collins pulled him to the outside and he began to make up some ground. Then a horse bumped him hard on his left side, throwing him off stride. By the time Jimmy got him corrected he had lost a significant amount of ground.

When they turned for home, the leader had pulled away from the field, but Crimson Delight was in the middle of the track, a clear path ahead of him.

By the eighth pole he was in sixth, by the sixteenth pole he was in third. As they crossed the wire he had managed to stick his nose out. He finished second in a photo finish.

Alex glanced up to where Laurel was sitting. She gave her a thumbs up.

When Jimmy came back he jumped off Delight. "I don't think I'd put him in a claiming race next time."

Alex couldn't help herself. She grabbed the jockey and gave him a big hug, almost lifting him off the ground.

Bobby placed the lead shank on Delight. "Jimmy, I don't know what she'll do if you win the next race," he grinned.

When they got back to the barn, Bobby walked Delight to cool him out while Cal and Alex got Feather ready for her race. "How's your nerves?" Cal asked.

"I still feel them, but I'm okay. I still can't believe the courage Delight showed."

"I'll have to say I'm a little surprised too," Cal answered.

Soon they were on their way to the paddock again. Alex was certain there needed to be two shanks on Feather, after the disaster in the gate with her last race. She had taken Feather to the gate numerous times for practice, but still she was not sure what to expect from the excitable filly. She was thankful Feather had drawn a post near the outside. Less time to stand in the gate, but with her early speed she would have to clear the field to get to the rail, the shortest route to the finish line.

The field broke without a hitch and Feather had no trouble in gaining the lead. It was just a matter of who could catch her now. Feather had recovered from her accident in record time, but Alex would have liked to have one more work in her before she raced. If she didn't win this race it would at least be a tightener for her next race which would be at Keeneland. That's where Laurel wanted to win a race.

Feather was still in the lead by mid-stretch, but another filly was closing fast. Could Feather hold out. The filly fought to hold the lead.

"Come on wire!" Alex screamed. "Don't hit her, Jimmy! She'll stop."

Feather gave her last lunge. They all thought it was enough for the win and they rushed toward the winner's circle, only to see the photo go up on the infield screen. Feather had lost by inches.

"Two seconds aren't bad," Bobby said as he put his arm around Alex's shoulders.

She shrugged him off. "A first would have been better."

The only consolation was what Jimmy said when he got back. "She'll win at Keeneland. I'll guarantee it."

Demon had never been on the turf track before, but again it was Cal who insisted they try it for his first race. "His pedigree and his big foot say he's a turf horse."

"Why not?" Alex asked herself. "He's not going to do anything anyway."

Alex never guessed she would soon be eating those words. From the start Demon went to the lead. As each of the horses came to him he seemed to gain more energy. He was determined to outrun his foes.

Alex uttered not a word as the race unfolded. Demon was pulling farther and farther away as they headed down the home stretch. Jimmy never had to even cock the whip. Demon was doing everything on his own. His official winning margin was eight lengths. He had led all the way.

Cal looked at his stop watch. "He's just two ticks off the track record," he yelled.

"Thank God I listened to you, Cal, and put him on the turf. He's a different horse on the grass."

"I think you can thank Barney. He came to me in a dream a couple of nights ago. He told me to insist Demon run on the grass."

A few days after the races at Churchill, Delight had a noticeable limp. Alex's vet called the clinic in Lexington. When they went over him the doctors found a chip in his ankle. After a call to Laurel it was decided that the chip had to be removed. It would be at least sixty days before he could resume training.

They were driving back to Louisville when Alex finally broke the silence. "It never stops—all these injuries. Why can't we have smooth sailing, at least for a little while?"

"You've got two horses to get ready for the Fall meet at Keeneland. Let's concentrate on them," Bobby answered.

"You're right. We need to count the blessing we have, not bemoan what's gone wrong."

Feather was entered the first week of the Keeneland meet. She was still nervous in the gate, but she catapulted out and within a few jumps she was a full two lengths in front of the field. Stunned, they watched the race unfold. By the time Feather reached the head of the stretch she was ten lengths in front and just galloping home.

Alex, Bobby, Cal, Laurel and John met up in the winner's circle. Alex was visibly shaking. Laurel grabbed her. "Good job," she grinned. "You've just fulfilled a dream of mine. Thank you so much."

"It's you I should thank, for giving me this chance. I don't think anyone else would have done that for me."

Laurel and John made their way to a quiet place after the winning photos were taken. Soon they were joined by a man neither of them knew. They couldn't believe the offer he made.

"Two hundred and fifty thousand is a lot of money," John said after the man had left. "You've got a lot of guts to turn him down."

"Feather will make us a lot more than that," Laurel smiled.

Alex took Cal up on his offer. "I'll get Demon ready and you go relax."

She sat down in the grass and guzzled her Diet Coke. Then she propped up her knees, buried her face in her arms and sobbed uncontrollably. It was a release of tears for utter joy.

Bobby and Cal led Demon to the paddock while Alex quietly followed. She went through the motions of saddling the colt. Then Jimmy Collins appeared. "I'm ready for my second win of the day," he quipped.

"We're ready too," Cal answered.

Demon was entered in an allowance race for non-winners of two races. His race was filled with royally bred colts, but Demon certainly didn't know it. Confidently, he looked around at his foes as they circled the walking ring. When he had seen each one, he gave an unexpected buck, his hind legs barely missing the walker in back of him.

Laurel and John were under the stands, watching on the TV screen, when Laurel whispered to John. "I think we need to move closer to the winner's circle. With that buck, he's just told us he's going to win."

Demon's race was not as easy for him as Feather's was. This time he was not able to go to the front, but stalked the leaders while in fourth place. Midway in the final turn Jimmy Collins eased him out. It didn't bother Jimmy that they would have to go wide. He knew he had a lot of horse under him.

Demon was flying down the center of the track. He seemed determined to pass the three horses in front of him. He passed the tiring third, then the second place horse. Now he took dead aim on the leader. The other jockey heard a horse coming after him and hit his mount right handed. For a moment Demon slowed. The opposing jockey's whip had grazed him on his nose. But quickly Demon seemed to focus again and with ears pinned back he made a final effort. When they crossed the finish line a half-length in front, Jimmy raised his whip high in the air. Never once had he hit Demon.

After the November meet at Churchill, Alex, Bobby, Cal and Laurel would have to decide what to do with the racing stable during the coming winter months. Laurel had asked if they needed to hole up during the winter at some training center since Churchill would close at the end of the meet and not open till the last of March.

"Not if we want to aim for the big races early next Spring," Alex responded. "We've got to keep them fit. There are three places we could go for the winter as I see it…Florida, Louisiana or Arkansas. I'd like to go to Arkansas where we could really test the horses in the tougher races. The California three-year-olds will be there and in the past couple of years they've done well in the Spring races in Kentucky."

"Whoa, wait a minute," Laurel interjected. "Are you thinking we might have some stakes horses?"

"I think Feather won't go the distance of the Oaks, but there are some sprint stakes and the Breeders Cup is at Churchill this next fall. If she keeps going the way she is now, I'll enter her in the Breeders Cup Sprint."

"There are some good turf races for Demon in Kentucky this spring," Bobby added.

Cal had remained quiet but now he spoke up. "I've been thinking. I believe Demon just might be able to run on the dirt too. What if we train him to run in the preps for the Kentucky Derby?"

Oaklawn Race Track in Hot Springs, Arkansas, was the place agreed on for them to race during the winter. Feather, Delight and Demon all turned three years old on January first, and Alex believed both Feather and Demon would be ready when Oaklawn opened in mid-January. Delight would be ready sometime in February. There were two prep races before the Arkansas Derby and if Demon did well in those races he would go into the Kentucky Derby as one of the favorites. There are a lot of IFs in racing, but optimism reigns supreme.

Then too, Ari offered to find them lodging, assuring them she knew the perfect place, a cottage on the lake.

It was Bobby who threw cold water on the plans. "If we go to Arkansas who will take care of the broodmares here at Alex's farm. I don't really want to stay here."

"No, no," Alex responded. "We're not going to break up our team. Surely we'll find the answer to the problem."

That answer came a few days later. Alex and Bobby had been asked to share dinner with Cal and Maria. They had just finished eating when a knock came at the front door.

Cal leaned back in his chair where he could see through the glass on the door. "It's John...and Lenny's with him. "Wonder what's up?" he frowned.

John Miller did not wait long before he answered Cal's question. "Lenny has a proposition he'd like to make you."

Lenny took a deep breath. "I'm so ashamed and so sorry for what I did to your barn, Alex. I've been trying to think of a way I could repay you for not filing charges against me. So...I'm wondering if you'd trust me enough to take care of your broodmares while you're in Arkansas."

Cal squirmed in his chair, but he settled down when Maria laid her hand on his arm. Alex caught Bobby's eye and he simply shrugged his shoulders. "Not my call," he said.

"I'll help Lenny keep an eye on things," John assured them.

"Lenny," Alex began, "there have been times people have given me a second chance." She glanced at Bobby.

"Me, too," he whispered.

"I see no reason for us not to give you a chance to make right what you did by setting the barn on fire. I'll pay you to take care of the horses."

"No, no," Lenny quickly replied. "I don't want to be paid. Just pay for their feed. I'll do the labor."

"I'll set up an account with the feed store," Alex said. "And thank you so much, Lenny."

Maria noticed the tears in Lenny's eyes as he and John turned to leave. "Everything will be fine," she said as the two men shut the front door behind them. "And...just to be sure I'll keep an eye on Lenny, too."

"That will keep him in line for sure," Cal laughed.

But before they left for Arkansas there was the November meet at Churchill. They had only to find races for Demon and Feather. Then they would move to Arkansas in December.

Jimmy Collins left his house before dawn. Normally he loved the crisp air of a November morning in Kentucky, but on this morning he shivered as he pulled his jacket around him. He put the heater on high and headed toward the interstate. He was scheduled to work several horses at Churchill, two of whom belonged to Alex.

Jimmy knew he never wanted to lose the mount on Feather. She was undoubtedly one of the best horses he'd ever ridden. But he had a call on an undefeated horse in the small stake Demon was scheduled for at Churchill.

Should he give up the mount on the horse that was sure to be the favorite in order to ride Demon? Jimmy had been on Demon for his works before he ever ran, and he knew the horse had some quirks about him. Jimmy wondered if those two wins for the horse were only flukes. He'd have to give Alex his answer this morning.

As his truck sped along the highway, Jimmy reminded himself of just how thankful he was to be able to ride again. Only a year ago a horse went down with him in a race. He sustained a concussion and a badly sprained wrist, but the rider beside him hadn't been so lucky. He was only a kid and now his life was over. When his horse went down he was dragged under the slashing hoofs. He didn't make it to the hospital.

That's when things reached a critical point in Jimmy's marriage. He understood how his wife felt, not knowing when a ride would be her husband's last. As he got older and the aches and pains became more evident, her anxiety increased. When Jimmy made the decision he was going to ride again after his injury, she filed for divorce. And their only child headed off to college several states away. Jimmy Collins was now alone in an empty house.

The first couple of months were the toughest. Even the slightest noise he made echoed through the house. To survive he knew he had to use that silence in some way to his benefit. Though he never thought he would ever do it, he began to meditate. The process soon began to give him a peacefulness, something he realized he had never experienced in his life.

As the warmth of the truck's heater relaxed Jimmy, he went into what he called his quiet space. Then out of the blue he heard a voice. It wasn't loud but it was very distinct. "Pull over when you come to the rest area."

He argued back. "What am I supposed to do, pull into the rest area and just sit there. Someone's bound to think I'm going to rob them or something worse."

The voice repeated its words, and Jimmy Collins did pull into the rest stop. He had a magazine beside him on the seat. He picked it up and began to stare at it as if he were reading while waiting on someone.

The five minutes he sat there seemed like an eternity. Suddenly he felt as if it were okay to drive on. "Damn voice," he said as he pulled back on to the interstate.

Just a mile down the road was a lighted traffic sign. "Multiple vehicle wreck ahead. Detour...."

Jimmy caught his breath. "If I hadn't pulled over...."

He turned off the interstate and made his way to a street that led to the track. It was then he heard the voice again. "Ride Demon," it said.

"Whatever you say," Jimmy answered out loud.

CHAPTER FORTY-SEVEN

REVIEWING

Laurel and Ari had fallen into a routine with the writing of Laurel's new book about the Miller farm. They met on Tuesday mornings, went over Ari's latest research, then Laurel would write after Ari left. But this morning was a bit different, Laurel realized, because Ari lingered. Something was on her mind.

"You've done wonderful research," Laurel nudged her.

"I simply love doing it."

Laurel pushed. "This must be quite a shock for you, falling into this crazy place with all the weird stuff that goes on here."

Ari choked back the tears. "This place and all of you have frankly saved my life. She composed herself. "But can I ask you something totally unrelated? Why do you name all your horses Crimson something?"

Laurel took a deep breath. "It was something my father used to talk about all the time."

Now Ari pushed for an answer. "I've never heard you speak about your father."

"Growing up was one of the most glorious times of my life. My father was a sports reporter for the *Washington Post*. One of his assignments was covering Thoroughbred racing. He used to take me to the track with him. He always talked about a horse he saw run several times. His name was Crimson Satan. That's why I use the Crimson name, to honor my father."

"At least you had an honorable one, unlike Lucien Caulder, my father."

"The same man who fathered my grandson, Cade," Laurel added. "But I have such admiration for Jane, your real mother. How difficult it must have been for her, having to give you up."

Ari nodded in agreement. "I couldn't have imagined how difficult until she told me about her horrible mother. Just imagine keeping all those feelings repressed for so many years."

"That's one of the most amazing things about Belle Rouge," Laurel smiled. "Anytime anyone comes in contact with it, their secrets are revealed. All the way from the Kilgores, the original owners, down to us."

"But it feels like burdens have been lifted when those secrets come out from hiding," Ari added.

"Do you sense anything about the Miller farm? Do you feel it wants to reveal its secrets?" Laurel asked.

"I do," came the answer. "Just look at what we learned about Rose. I think about her all the time and how strong she was. How I admire that little girl who was dispersed on the train during the Civil War. The two sons she had with Preston Miller seemed to be strong too. That strength was passed down through their sons to your husband John's father, but not to Jane's father. Why did he marry that horrible woman who was so mean to Jane, her own daughter? I know Jane was so thankful she had her grandmother."

"By the way, have you found out anything about Jane's grandmother?" Laurel asked. "Who she was, how she became acquainted with the Miller family?"

"Not yet," Ari shrugged. "It seems she's as much a mystery as Rose was."

"I'm wondering if Rose played any part in choosing her to marry her son."

"I don't know, Laurel, but I think that will be my project for this coming week—finding out who Jane's grandmother really was."

"And I think her identity is very important to this current book I'm writing."

Still Ari lingered and Laurel waited.

Finally, Ari continued. "I simply can't believe what comes about when each of us comes in contact with Belle Rouge. Besides secrets coming out, relationships are mended. There's Alex's learning that Viola is her sister. Alex and Bobby's finding each other again after all their years apart. Why didn't they get together in high school?"

"Ari," Laurel answered, "sometimes it takes a lot of life experiences to make people see things or people differently. Bobby had to experience going to college, teaching and really getting bored with his life for him to see he really did belong here in the country and with Alex. Jane was afraid she'd interfere with your life if she tried to find you. It took your searching to find her that brought you two together."

"I can see that," Ari answered, "and I know this is none of my business, but are you okay with finding out that Lenny is the son of your husband?"

"Strangely, I am."

Still Ari continued. "And it's so amazing that Cal, a descendant of Barney, a slave of the Kilgores, ended up here on the very farm where Barney lived. And what a burden Viola carried, knowing that Alex was her sister and she just couldn't bring herself to tell her."

Laurel twisted in her chair. "I think there is a lot more to their story than even they know."

"Is that yet another book?" Ari grinned.

"There are many stories yet to be told," Laurel answered. "And there's one I'm a little afraid to tell John. Beth has asked me to go with her to North Carolina. Her father wants to see Cade. His marriage didn't work out and I think he's lonely. And one of my friends there wants me to talk with her book club about Belle Rouge. I also think I need to mend some fences with Beth's father. The problem is, I know John can't go with me. He has to go to some statewide meeting of law enforcement officers.

The thing he will object to most is that Beth and Cade are going to stay for a week and I'll be driving back by myself."

CHAPTER FORTY-EIGHT

WHAT IS TIME?

The day was waning when Laurel turned onto the road that led to Belle Rouge. She finally felt as if she were home, but leaving North Carolina had been a difficult decision. She and Beth's father had a full blown argument, each blaming the other for the divorce. Then there was Beth's decision to stay with her father.

"Funny," Laurel thought, "how even the smallest happening can totally change the direction of one's life. But sometimes we are forced to make decisions." When she had made the decision to move to Cedarville, Kentucky, and to buy Belle Rouge, her life made a radical shift.

Laurel slowly made the turn into the driveway of her new home. She eased the black SUV between the two pillars that flanked the entrance and unsnapped her seatbelt at the same time.

At first she hadn't seen the car coming down the drive and heading toward her. It came at her out of the shadows of the trees. Then things seemed to move in slow motion. Questions popped into her mind. *Why had she unsnapped her seat belt? Why wasn't the oncoming car slowing down. She had her foot on the brake. Why wasn't the other car stopping?*

Then she felt the jarring thud as the oncoming car hit the driver's side fender of her car. Again she asked herself, "Why did I unfasten my seatbelt?"

The crash threw Laurel to her right, but with her foot applying the brake she was also catapulted toward the windshield.

For an instant she saw the other driver. She would never forget him. His hair was black and curly, but it was the sneer on his face that she knew would stay with her, etched in her mind. There was the hideous crunch of metal as his car hit the pillar on her left. His car folded onto him like an accordion. Laurel knew she had just seen a man die. And in her heart she knew he had hit her on purpose. *But why?*

Then Laurel's head hit the windshield. She felt the heat from the blow move through her body. There was a moment of blackness. Then she was awake.

Why wasn't she feeling any pain, she asked herself? Then she realized she was not fully awake. She could not move her body, yet her mind was more aware than she had ever experienced.

People were gathering around her. One man stood out. He was tall. His badge caught a bit of the last light of the day. Then it was as if she began to hover above the accident scene. The man in the other car was dead. She knew it. Crimson blood flowed from his face. It was the same color as the leaves on the trees, she noted. Her car was braced against the other pillar. "How ironic," she thought. "One pillar killed him and the other saved me."

She heard someone's voice ask the tall man a question. "Who's the dead man?"

"It's Lucien Caulder," came the reply.

CHAPTER FORTY-NINE

WHO IS SHE?

Laurel remembered bits and pieces of what happened next. She remembered being lifted from her wrecked car, being placed in the ambulance. She shook in the cold. Then she remembered being placed in a bed, tubes, needles, machines and various people in white, in blue. She heard the word "concussion."

She saw a shadow in her doorway. "Dr. Nila," she smiled to herself. A tall man followed the doctor into the room.

"Has she come to yet, Dr. Nila?" he asked.

"No," she answered. "And it's quite puzzling. The concussion was mild and she should have awakened by now."

"What do you plan to do next," the man asked.

"There's something I've already done," came the reply. "I phoned a couple of colleagues where I used to work. There was a case similar to this in Savannah when I was there. And another one in Santa Fe when I was there. They each had a case where the patient took a long time to become fully awake after a relatively mild concussion. They told me they really had no explanation as to why. They just diagnosed it as a virus."

The man stepped to where Laurel could see him. "John," she realized.

He was speaking. "Well, we at least know who she is and why she was in Cedarville. Seems as though she had just purchased Belle Rouge."

"Sheriff, have you been able to contact any relatives?" the doctor asked.

"Yes, her daughter will be here tomorrow. She's driving in from North Carolina. And my cousin recognized your patient's name. It's Laurel Mackenzie. She's a writer."

"Here's what I'm going to do, Sheriff Miller. I'm asking some of the volunteers to come in and sit with her around the clock. I want them to observe everything Ms. Mackenzie does: every movement, every eye blink. And I'm asking a friend of mine, Professor Robert Ferguson who teaches psychology at the university, to consult with me on this case. The volunteers will start today. And by the way, your cousin Jane and her friends Eva and Viola are the ones who will be doing this. Oh, there is one more, Alex Jardine."

"Yes, I know her," the sheriff replied. "She trains horses. But I can't imagine her volunteering to sit with a patient."

"As you probably know, Ms. Jardine lives close to Belle Rouge. She was at the wreck site and then she came to me. She said she felt compelled to help, so I asked her if she could do a shift of sitting with my patient. She said she was thrilled to do so. "Funny," Dr. Nila smiled. "I find it a bit strange she used the word 'compelled.' I was just happy to know she was able to fill the final slot in our schedule."

As Beth exited the elevator at the hospital she saw a group of people gathered at the nurses' station. A tall mulatto woman came toward her.

"I'm Dr. Nila," the woman said. "You're Ms. Mackenzie's daughter?"

"Yes," Beth replied. "I'm sorry it took so long to find any of the family, but Dad's out of the country on vacation. The authorities couldn't find anyone at our house, but on the second attempt, a neighbor told them I was attending Duke. Is Mom okay?"

"Let's go to a conference room," Dr. Nila responded. "I want to introduce you to some people. And to answer your question. Your mother is doing well physically."

Beth was puzzled. There was something in Dr. Nila's voice. She knew there was a lot more to learn about her mother's condition.

Dr. Nila began the introductions. To my left is Viola Flowers and next to her are Jane Miller and Eva Farnsworth. To my right are Alex Jardine and Dr. Robert Ferguson, a colleague of mine. I've also asked the sheriff to meet with us as he was one of the first on the scene of the accident. He'll be here in a few minutes."

"But," the doctor continued, "first, Beth, I want to explain some things about your mother's condition."

Beth felt her body tense.

"Your mother had a concussion. It wasn't severe, but for some reason she hasn't regained consciousness. I'm going to admit to you I don't know why. That's why I called in Dr. Ferguson. He's a psychologist and I thought he could shed some light on the situation. Dr. Ferguson, will you explain your thoughts on the situation?"

"I'm sorry we couldn't meet in a more pleasant way, Miss Mackenzie. But sometimes, and I'm not going to use the word 'coma' in your mother's case, a person will not immediately regain consciousness after a trauma. We don't always know why. Medicine still has a long way to go in the study of the human brain. Please know that I'm not trying to scare you. I do believe your mother will eventually be completely healed. It just may take some time."

"Beth," Dr. Nila interjected, "After your mother was here a few days it appeared as if she were going to regain consciousness. We knew she was on the verge of doing so, but she just couldn't do it. That's when Dr. Ferguson and I decided to ask these women to come and sit with her in shifts. We asked them to talk with her as if she could hear them. Viola, could you fill Beth in on what you experienced?"

"Yes, thank you. Both Dr. Nila and Dr. Ferguson are open to alternative forms of medicine. I know it's a bit odd for them to call me in because I'm a psychic. I sense things. And I feel I've been able to make a connection with your mother. I think she's afraid to wake up. It's as if, and I hesitate to say this, but of course I will, she has seen something she doesn't want to face. I know that's strange, but that's the only way I can explain it."

Dr. Ferguson spoke up. "Beth, in my experience, I've known other people like Viola. We don't know why they have these abilities, but sometimes they are spot on."

Alex interjected. "I think I can speak for Jane and me. We just sat beside Laurel and talked with her as if she could hear us. I don't claim to be psychic like Viola, but I felt she liked hearing about my horses."

Beth fought back tears. "Mom loves horses. It would be one of the highlights of her life if she had one to race at Churchill Downs. She talked about it often before she left North Carolina."

Now it was Jane who spoke up. "May I ask why Laurel came here?"

"Mom wanted to start over. She and Dad divorced and my father already had a girlfriend. That's why he's in Europe right now. He and his new wife are on their honeymoon. It isn't that Mom still loved him. Sometimes I wonder if they ever did love one another. They were so opposite."

Beth continued. "One day Mom just announced she wanted to move to Kentucky where her great-grandparents once lived. She phoned me—it had to be the morning of her accident—and said she thought she had found a farm to buy."

A voice came from the direction of the doorway. "She was turning into Belle Rouge when a car that was coming out crashed into her."

"Beth, let me introduce Sheriff Miller, Jane's cousin. He was first on the scene of your mother's accident."

The sheriff sat down across from Beth. "You said your mother phoned you. Did she have a cell phone?"

Beth nodded.

"That's strange," Miller continued. "We thought she might but we couldn't find it. That's why it took us several days to find any of her family. We also didn't find a purse, but we did find a card belonging to a real estate firm."

"Mom did have an agent looking online for property here in Cedarville."

Dr. Nila rose from her chair. "Now let me take you to see your mother."

As Dr. Nila and Beth stood at Laurel's bedside, the doctor spoke. "I might not go into as much detail about a patient's condition as I'm going to with you, Beth. When we contacted your college they mentioned that you're in pre-med at Duke."

"I am," Beth responded. "I don't know in which field I'll concentrate, but I wouldn't be surprised if my mother's case didn't direct me."

"Good," Dr. Nila patted her shoulder. "Let's start from the time she was admitted to the hospital. The patient most certainly had a concussion as the tests confirmed. However, she wasn't regaining consciousness as quickly as we thought she would."

"For the next three days the brain was less active. Truthfully, I was becoming alarmed. Then this morning there was increased activity. To be honest, Beth, I don't quite understand why she hasn't regained consciousness. There's no physical reason why she shouldn't."

Beth reached out and took Laurel's hand. "Dr. Nila, our professor took us on a field trip to a hospital. He wanted us to see some of the case studies they were doing. There was a patient who had the same condition as my mother. They were puzzled too. They deduced it was some sort of a virus."

"My colleagues came to the same conclusion. That's a rather odd diagnosis, but I think it might be the best we can do," Dr. Nila said. "Beth, I think she might respond to your voice. Just talk to her about anything that comes to mind. The rest of us want to stay for a while to see if Laurel responds. I'll finish my rounds and the others will be just across the hall."

The volunteers knew they might be in for a long wait. Viola chose a chair in the corner of the room. She closed her eyes and went into a deep meditation. Jane spoke to Eva. "Are you alright? You're very pale."

Dr. Ferguson asked Alex to accompany him out into the hall.

"It's been a long time," he said.

"I know," Alex answered. "I don't think I've seen you but a couple of times since we graduated from high school. Our paths certainly went in different directions. You've come a long way in your profession. But I certainly haven't."

"I've seen you a couple of times in the winner's circle at Churchill," Dr. Ferguson responded.

"Very few," Alex said.

Robert Ferguson surprised himself. "Do you think we could have dinner sometime?"

Beth had been at her mother's bedside for just under half an hour when the sheriff came back into the room.

"I thought you might want to hear about the circumstances of your mother's accident," he said.

"Yes, please."

"On the day of the accident your mother had contacted a local real estate agent, and he was supposed to meet her at the farm called Belle Rouge. He was delayed and she got there first. She was making a left hand turn into the drive when another car came speeding down the drive toward her. He hit her car on the driver's side front fender. I'm afraid she wasn't wearing her seatbelt."

"Mom did that every time she pulled into our drive at home. It drove me nuts."

Sheriff Miller continued. "Your mother was lucky. The pillar on her right kept her from spinning and maybe from rolling over."

"Was the man drinking?" Beth asked.

"He was a little over the legal limit."

"And who was he?" Beth asked. "Why was he speeding down a driveway?"

"His name was Lucien Caulder and he wasn't exactly an upstanding character. He always claimed he was entitled to ownership of Belle Rouge. My guess is that he heard your mother was going to purchase the farm and he wanted to stop her."

A movement on the screen beside Laurel's bed caught Sheriff Miller's eye. "Something is happening," he said.

"Get Dr. Nila," Beth ordered. "I think Mom is waking up!"

It was late into the evening when Laurel awoke, this time from a restful sleep. "Have you been here all afternoon, Beth?" she asked.

"Yes," she answered. "I've been reading and dozing."

"Is Dr. Nila coming in tonight?"

"She should be here any minute, Mom."

"Did I hear my name?" Dr. Nila asked. "And how is my favorite patient?"

"I'm feeling much stronger," Laurel responded.

"We had quite an afternoon," Dr. Nila smiled. "The people who have been sitting with you have all come back and they are waiting to come in and see you. But Laurel, I want to ask you something first. When you first awoke you were asking about Eva. I don't understand how you knew there was somebody here named Eva. You kept saying she needed to get to the doctor."

"Did she get checked out?"

"Yes. Jane and Viola took your demand very seriously because Eva had not been feeling well. She's been admitted to the hospital and she was diagnosed with a blood clot. But thanks to your warning, she'll recover. Jane is sitting with her and I'm sure she'll be fine. I just don't know how you knew something was wrong with her."

"I'll try to explain later, but I'm so happy she's okay" Laurel said. "And now I have a request. Will you ask Viola to stay for a while? And I know you're a busy doctor, but if you could stay, too...."

"I'm off duty and I can tell you I'd like to have a listen to what you have to say. And Dr. Ferguson and Alex want to take Beth to get some rest. She'll stay with Alex Jardine," Dr. Nila reported.

"That's good," Laurel said. "They need to get to know one another."

Dr. Nila and Viola gave a questioning glance at one another. Then they pulled their chairs close to Laurel's bedside and waited for her to speak.

Laurel took a deep breath and began. "I know you might think I'm out of my mind with what I'm about to say, but I have to tell you what has been going on in my head since the accident."

"I remember seeing the other car just before it crashed into my car. But I did get a good look at the driver of the other car. I'm not at all sure that he didn't hit me on purpose."

"Let me stop you right here, Laurel," Dr. Nila said. "Sheriff Miller has the same suspicion. He'll be here in a couple of hours to discuss it with you. Now please continue, and do you mind if I take notes?"

"Not at all," Laurel assured her. "Especially if what I'm about to tell you will help in some way with other patients."

Laurel continued. "I know now I was in the hospital the entire time, but I feel as if I've been other places too. I understand that it was my mind doing it, but nevertheless, it's very real to me."

Laurel told her story. At first it was as if she had been allowed to see into the past of Belle Rouge. She saw what had happened to the Kilgores, the original owners. She described the terrible tragedies that struck the family. There was a special man on the farm, a man named Barney who tried to take care of Claire Kilgore. His wife Genevieve was a terrible person. She learned that Claire was not the daughter of Sumner Kilgore, but that she was conceived as a result of his wife's affair with the doctor who was Eva's ancestor. Laurel also learned she was a descendant of Claire, whose child had been adopted by the family who took her to North Carolina.

Then years seemed to fly by. She saw herself involved with the man who traced his ancestry back to Barney's wife who had been the mistress of Sumner Kilgore. This man, Lucien Caulder, had convinced himself he was the rightful heir to the farm.

"But that part can't be true," Laurel told them. "He was just killed in the accident."

"We'll talk about that later," Viola said. "Please just relate what you saw while you were unconscious."

Laurel was elated that neither Dr. Nila nor Viola made light of what she had revealed to them. She was eager to continue. "Then there was a respite. I saw nothing for a while."

Dr. Nila responded. "That must explain what we saw on the screen. I will tell you I was very concerned at that time. We simply didn't know what was happening. First there was a lot of brain activity and then, hardly a thing. This must have been your time of respite."

"I had no concept of time," Laurel said. "I saw what had happened in the past, and now I have to find out if what I saw was the truth. Honestly, I've had writer's block for some time and my agent has been prodding me to get started on another book. I now know that book will be about the Kilgores of Belle Rouge."

Laurel took a deep breath then began again. "After a while I'm sure I saw something else. I'm certain I saw into the future."

When Laurel finished Dr. Nila rose to go. "What an amazing story. And to think you remembered it in such detail. I think that is the difference between you and other patients who have been in a coma. You were able to remember such details. But I must go now. I have an early shift tomorrow, however I doubt I'll get much sleep. I feel as if I've had the privilege of seeing something very few doctors have seen or heard. Thank you, Laurel. And," she added, "Sheriff Miller phoned just before I came to your room. All he said was that there had been an incident this afternoon and it would be a while before he could get here to ask you your version of your accident."

Laurel asked Viola if she could stay for a while. She wasn't quite ready to be alone and besides there were some more things she needed to tell someone. It felt to her that Viola would understand what she was about to reveal....

Before she could begin, Viola said, "You were a bit reluctant to say some things in front of the doctor."

"Yes," Laurel answered. "What I've experienced these past days wasn't a dream as I told them. And I could hear every word you and the others said as you sat with me. Alex talked about her horses. Then she spoke about talking with Dr. Ferguson for the first time since they graduated from high school. She spoke of her plans to try to get some really good horses. I now know I'll be buying her some horses and we'll do well."

"Laurel, we were all told to talk to you as if you could carry on a conversation with us. I'm just curious. What do you remember my telling you?"

"That Alex is your sister and she doesn't know it and that you believe you might have a half-brother. You really do need to tell her."

"Yes, I know. I just have to look for the right time. I'm afraid it will drive her away when she finds out that I've kept it from her all these years."

The two women were quiet for a moment, each lost in her own thoughts. Then Laurel giggled.

"What is it?" Viola grinned.

"I was also allowed to look into the future a bit. I think Sheriff Miller and I have a pretty good future together."

"Yes, I noticed something between you two when he was here. Care to share?"

"Not yet."

Again there was silence. This time it was broken by Viola. "So, where does Laurel Mackenzie go from here? I hope you're not contemplating buying Belle Rouge. It would take a fortune to do all the repairs it needs."

"I'm comfortable with the settlement I got from the divorce and my books have sold very well. Besides I've already signed a contract to buy the property."

"Then you plan to stay here?"

"I would love that. I certainly feel as if I know all of you personally, if that's possible."

"You had a strange, but wonderful introduction to all of us. Laurel, is there something you're not telling me?"

"It's about Jane. She told me something terribly personal when she thought I couldn't hear her."

"About the child she gave up?"

Laurel nodded. "She told me the father's name. It was the man who crashed into my car."

"Oh, dear God. I never suspected that. I thought it was someone she met in college."

"I'm afraid she'll be scared off when she knows just how much I remember about her story."

"Why don't you talk with her privately, Laurel. I know she's so grateful you told her Eva needed to see a doctor. They've been best friends for a long time."

"So," Viola said, "nothing could have persuaded you to buy a different property?"

"No. I belong at Belle Rouge. But I do think with that man's dying in the wreck, the story might just differ a bit from what I saw when I was unconscious."

Viola leaned closer and whispered. "When we are privileged to see into the future we can stop things from happening. From everything you've told us about Lucien Caulder, the future may change quite a bit with his being killed in the wreck."

Laurel could feel a tear trickle down her cheek. "But something wonderful did happen because of Lucien Caulder. He fathered my exceptional grandson, Cade. What if Cade never comes along?"

"Don't worry about that," Viola assured her. That boy will find a way to come to us. I predict that Beth will find a marvelous husband. Besides, you didn't see far enough into the future to tell if Cade ever picked up any of Lucien Caulder's traits."

"Viola, I feel so guilty about his dying."

"No, no, it was his doing. He was trying to harm you. You were his intended victim. In no way were you at fault. Everyone knows the evil he had in his heart. And if your vision into the past at Belle Rouge is correct, he inherited a lot from his ancestor, Genevieve."

"Viola, do you think it's possible I could have a baby?"

Before Viola could answer, a figure appeared in the doorway. She quickly changed the subject. "You look beat."

"It's been quite an afternoon," the sheriff replied. "One of my deputies had some sort of a breakdown when he heard about the wreck. Today we had to put him into a mental facility."

"Oh, my word!" Viola exclaimed.

"He'll be okay when he learns the truth," Laurel said before she had time to think.

"What do you mean?" the sheriff frowned. Then he glanced at Viola. "I thought you were our local psychic."

"I have company now," Viola laughed. "Oh, Laurel has seen a lot more things while she was in the coma, or whatever it was. Now I'm sure you two have some business to discuss, so I'll head for home."

"Thank you, Viola." Laurel called after her. Then she turned to the sheriff. "Take a deep breath," she said.

Sheriff Miller leaned back in the chair and closed his eyes for a moment. Laurel studied him. He wasn't the handsomest of men, at least not like her former husband. But she was happy for that. Her husband was vain, a flirt and totally self-absorbed. Miller was the type of man who wouldn't stray from marriage vows. She just knew it. Laurel closed her eyes, wondering if what she had seen was correct. Would she and the sheriff really get together? Then there was the matter of their having a child. She had seen that so clearly.

"Why are you grinning?" the sheriff smiled.

"Just thinking about the future," Laurel replied.

"Do you think Cedarville will be a part of your future?"

"Very much so," Laurel said, "and the people in it."

Miller didn't know if the events of the day made him let his guard down, but he heard himself say to her. "I think I really like that last part." He caught himself. "I mean…." he stuttered.

"I think I will like it too."

He leaned toward her. "So what are you going to do here, besides like the people?" he teased.

Laurel pondered the question, then she answered. "I'm going to have a successful racing stable, and I'm going to write more books. Some very interesting people are going to appear in our lives. And—I'm, that is—we're going to be very happy."

Sheriff Miller took her hand before he left. "I look forward to getting to know you, Laurel Mackenzie."

"Likewise," she smiled.

Laurel settled down after he left, letting herself relax. She realized just how tired she was. She was about to doze off when something popped into her mind. "Cal and Maria. They're not here."

From somewhere inside she heard a voice. "We'll be there soon."

Laurel drifted off. This time it was a different voice she heard. "I been waiting for you to come home, Miz Laurel."

"I'm here, Barney," Laurel whispered.

Joyce Farmer Trammell

www.ingramcontent.com/pod-product-compliance
Lightning Source LLC
Chambersburg PA
CBHW060642260626
47161CB00008B/2957